Everything about the moment felt forbidden...

And inevitable. She could feel her hair shifting back and forth along her shoulders as Brodie's hand swept along her back to her waist. The play of his fingers along the curves between her breasts and hips elicited hypersensitive tingles as if she were being lit up from within. If she had thought she knew what being touched by a man was like before, she knew for certain she'd had no idea until now. Each infinitesimal movement of Brodie's fingertips, hips, even his breath spoke to her very essence.

He untangled their fingers and tipped her chin up as he lowered his lips to meet hers. Tentative at first. A near chaste kiss. Then another. Longer, more inquisitive. His short beard was unbelievably soft. Kali's fingers crept up to trace along his jawline as his hands cupped hers. Her lips parted, wanting more than anything to taste and explore his full lips. A soft moan passed between the pair of them—she had no idea where it had started or how it had finished, she was only capable of surrendering to the onslaught of sensations. On her skin, inside her belly, shifting and warming, farther, deeper than she'd ever experienced. She felt delicate and protected in his arms. And utterly free to abandon herself to the erotic washes of heat and desire coursing through to her very core.

Dear Reader,

So good to see you here, about to embark on Kali and Brodie's journey to a Highland HEA. I enjoy writing all of my books, but this one really took hold of my imagination in the form of two different radio stories I heard. I'm a bit of a radio and podcast junkie and soak up stories whenever I'm in the car.

One was a story about an amazing young woman who had been tricked into a "summer break" in her parents' homeland only to discover it was an arranged marriage. She was rescued by a group who work with the British Embassy but on the condition she never see her family again. As you can imagine, that set the wheels turning.

Then I heard another story about some amazing doctors who, during the recent Ebola crisis in Africa, volunteered to go work with patients under pretty harrowing conditions only to discover, upon their return, reintegrating back into the patient-doctor world of the UK was a lot trickier than they'd anticipated. Cue: more reeling brain cogs.

Those are a lot of extenuating circumstances to deal with! What remains ever dazzling to me about falling in love, and the power of being in love, is what a person can overcome when they've found that special someone. This is one of those stories. I hope you enjoy Kali and Brodie's story, and please do feel free to get in touch no matter what you thought! There's absolutely no need to feel shy. I can be reached on Twitter, @AnnieONeilBooks, or at annie@annieoneilbooks.com.

Enjoy!

Annie O' x

Books by Annie O'Neil

Harlequin Medical Romance

Hot Latin Docs
Santiago's Convenient Fiancée

Christmas Eve Magic
The Nightshift Before Christmas

The Monticello Baby Miracles
One Night, Twin Consequences

Doctor...to Duchess?
One Night...with Her Boss
London's Most Eligible Doctor

Visit the Author Profile page
at Harlequin.com for more titles.

This book goes out to—and I'm stealing her
phrase here—the best friend I never met,
the marvelous Nettybean. She's ALWAYS there
for me and I am ever grateful. Thanks, Netts—
hope you don't mind having to go to an inclement
Scottish Island for a big slice of gratitude pie!

xx Annie O'

Praise for
Annie O'Neil

"This is a beautifully written story that will pull
you in from page one and keep you up late and
turning the pages."

—*Goodreads* on
Doctor…to Duchess?

**Annie O'Neil won the 2016 RoNA Rose Award
for her book *Doctor…to Duchess?***

CHAPTER ONE

NO AMOUNT OF torrential rain unforgivingly lashing his face would equal the storm brewing inside of Brodie McClellan. Not today. Not tomorrow. A month of Sundays wouldn't come close.

And yet he had to laugh…even though everything he was feeling was about as far off the spectrum of "funny ha-ha" as laughter could get. He'd seen death on a near daily basis for the months he'd been away, but this one…? This one had him soul-searching in the one place he'd longed to leave behind. *Blindsided* didn't even come close to what he was feeling.

"Hey, Dad."

He crouched low to the ground, unable to resist leveling out a small hillock of soft soil soaked through with the winter rains. The earth appeared months away from growing even a smattering of grass to cover his father's grave. It was no surprise that his brother hadn't come good on his promise to lay down some turf. It was difficult enough to drag him down from the mountains, let alone—

Enough. Callum had a good heart, and he had to be hurting, too.

Brodie dragged his fingers through the bare

earth again. Time would change it. Eventually. It would become like his mother's—the grave just to the left. The one he still couldn't bear to look at. He moved his fingers behind him, feeling long-established grass. A shocking contrast to the bare earth in front of him.

Yes, time would change it. Just as it had all the graves, each one protected with a thick quilt of green. Time he didn't have nor wanted to give to Dunregan. Not after all it had taken from him.

He scanned the parameters of the graveyard with a growing sense of familiarity. Brodie had spent more time here in the past fortnight than he had in a lifetime of growing up on the island. Asking, too late, for answers to all the questions he should have asked before he'd left Dunregan in his wake.

Gray. It was all he could see. Gray headstones. Gray skies. Gray stones making up the gray walls. A color washout.

He ran a hand across the top of his father's headstone. "We'll get this place fixed up for you, Father. All right? Put in some flowers or something."

A memory pinged into his head of Callum and himself, digging up snowdrop bulbs when he'd been just a young boy. His father counting out a few pence for each cluster. He swiped his face to clear off the rain, surprised to discover he was smiling at the memory of his paltry pocket money. The small towers of copper pennies had seemed like riches at the time.

"I'll get you some snowdrops, eh, Dad? Those'll be nice. And some bluebells later on? For you and Mum. She always loved bluebell season."

He shook his head when he realized he was waiting for an answer.

"It's a bit of a nightmare at the clinic. I've had to call in a locum. It'll buy me time until I figure out how to explain to folk that it's okay. *I'm* okay."

He looked up to the skies again, unsurprised to find his mood was still as turbulent as the weather. Wind was blowing every which where. Rain was coming in thick bursts. Cold. It was so ruddy *cold* up here on Dunregan.

He pressed his hands to his thighs, stood up and cursed softly. Mud. All over his trousers.

For the few minutes it took to drive home Brodie tried his best to plumb a good mood from somewhere in the depths of his heart. He wasn't this guy. This growling, frowning man whose image he kept catching in the rearview mirror. He was a loving son. Older sibling to a free-spirited younger brother. Cousin, nephew, friend. And yet he felt like a newcomer. A stranger amidst a sea of familiarity. A man bearing more emotional weight on his shoulders than he'd ever carried before.

He pulled the car into the graveled drive in front of the family home, only to jam the brakes on.

"What the—?"

Wood. A huge stack of timber filling the entire driveway. He'd barely spoken to anyone since he'd returned to Dunregan, let alone ordered a pile of wood!

Brodie jumped out of his four-by-four and searched for a delivery note. He found it tucked under a stack of quarter-inch plywood. His eyes scanned the paper. The list of cuts and types of wood all began to slot into place, take on form… build one very particular item.

The boat.

The boat he and his father had always promised they would build.

The one he'd never been able to think about after that day when he'd come home from sailing without his mother.

Another sharp sting of emotion hit and stuck in his throat.

Today.

All he had to do was get through today. And then tomorrow he'd do it all over again, and then one more time until the pain began to ebb, like the tides surrounding the island he'd once called home.

Kali's grip tightened on her handlebars.

The elements vs the cyclist.

Game on.

She lifted her head, only to receive a blast of

wind straight in the face. Her eyes streamed. Her nose was threatening to run. Her hair…? That pixie cut she'd been considering might've been a good idea. So much for windswept and interesting. Windswept and bedraggled was more like it—but she couldn't keep the grin off her face.

Starting over—*again*—was always going to be an uphill struggle, but she hadn't thought this particular life reboot would be so *physical*!

Only one hundred more meters between Mother Nature's finest blasts of Arctic wind and a hot cup of tea. Who would win? Fledgling GP? Or the frigid forces of Scotland's northernmost islands?

Another briny onslaught of wind and sea spray sent Kali perilously close to the ditch. A ditch full of…*ugh*. One glimpse of the ice-skinned murk convinced her to swing a leg off her vintage-style bicycle and walk. A blast of icy water shot up from her feet along her legs, giving her whole body a wiggle of chills. She looked down at the puddle her ballerina flats–clad feet had landed in.

Splatterville. A shopping trip for boots and a proper jacket might be in order. So much for the romantic idea of tootling along Dunregan's coast road and showing up to her first day of work with rosy-cheeked panache. There were tulips blooming all over the place in London! How long was it going to take the Isle of Dunregan to catch up?

"Dr. O'Shea?"

A cheery fifty-something woman rode up alongside her, kitted out in a thick waterproof jacket, boots, woolen mittens, hat…everything Kali should've been wearing but wasn't. Her green eyes crackled with mischief…or was that just the weather?

"Yes." Kali smiled, then grimaced as the wind took a hold of her facial features. She must look like some sort of rubber-lipped cartoon character by now!

"Ailsa Dunregan." She hopped off her bike and walked alongside Kali, and laughed when Kali's eyes widened. "Yes. I know, it's mad, isn't it? Same name as the island. Suffice it to say, my family—or at least my husband's family—has been here a long time. *My* family's only been here a few hundred years."

Hundred?

"How'd you know it was me?"

Ailsa threw back her head and laughed. The sound was instantly yanked away by the wind. "Only someone not from Dunregan would—"

Kali struggled to make out what she was saying, her own thoughts fighting with the wind and making nothing comprehensible.

"Sorry?" Kali tried to push her bike a bit closer and keep up the brisk pace the woman was setting.

"I'm the practice nurse!" Ailsa shouted against the elements. "I get all the gossip, same as the publican, and not too many people come to the island this time of year."

Kali nodded, only just managing to keep her bike upright with the approach of another gust.

"It has its merits!" Kali shouted back when she'd regained her footing.

"You think?" Ailsa hooted another laugh into the stratosphere. "If you're after a barren, desolate landscape…" she groaned as her own cycle was nearly whipped out of her hands "…you've come to the right place!"

As if by mutual agreement they both put their heads down, inching their cycles along the verge. Kali smiled into the cozy confines of her woolen scarf—her one practical nod to the subzero temperature. Compared to the other obstacles she'd faced, this one was easy-peasy. Just a healthy handful of meters between her and her new life.

No more hiding. No more looking over her shoulder. Okay, so she still had a different name, thanks to the heaven-sent Forced Marriage Protection Unit, and there were a boatload of other issues to deal with one day—but right here, right now, with the wind blowing more than the cobwebs away, she felt she really was Kali O'Shea. Correction! *Dr.* Kali O'Shea. Safe and sound on the uppermost Scottish Isle of Dunregan.

As if it had actual fingers, the frigid tempest abruptly yanked her bicycle out of her hands, sending her into a swan dive onto the rough pavement and the bicycle skidding into the ditch. The *deep* ditch. The one she'd have to clamber into and probably shred her tights.

She looked down at her knees as she pressed herself up from the pavement. Nope! That job was done already. *Nice one, Kali.* So much for renaming herself after the goddess of empowerment. The goddess of grace might've been a better choice.

"Oh, no! Are you all right, darlin'?" Ailsa was by her side in a minute.

Kali fought the prick of tears, pressing her hands to her scraped knees to regroup. *C'mon, Kali. You're a grown woman now.*

If only...

No. Focus on the positives. She didn't do "if onlys" anymore.

"What's going on here?"

A pair of sturdy leather boots appeared in Kali's eyeline. They must go with the rich Scottish brogue she was hearing.

"You pulling patients in off the streets now, Ailsa?"

Kali's eyes zipped up the long legs, skidded across the thick wax jacket and landed soundly on… Ooh… She'd never let herself think she had a type, but this walking, talking advert for a Scandi-Scottish fisherman type with…ooh, again!…the most beautiful cornflower-blue eyes…

She swallowed.

He might be it. There was something about him that said...*safe.*

Thirtyish? With a straw-blond thatch of hair and a strong jawline covered in facial hair a few days past designer stubble to match. She'd never thought she was one to go for a beardy guy, but with this weather suddenly it made sense. She wondered how it would feel against her cheek. Reassuringly scratchy or unexpectedly soft?

She blinked away the thought and refocused.

He was no city mouse. That was for sure. It wouldn't be much of a step to picture him on a classic motorbike, lone wolfing it along the isolated coastline. And he was tall. *Well...* Everyone was tall compared to her, but he had a nice, strong, mountain-climber thing going on. You didn't see too many men like that in London. Perhaps they were all hiding out here, in Scotland's subarctic islands, waiting to rescue city slickers taken out by the elements.

"All right, darlin'?" He put a hand on her shoulder, his eyes making a quick visual assessment, gave a satisfied nod and headed for the steep embankment. "Here, I'll just grab your bicycle for you."

Chivalrous to boot!

Strange how she didn't even know him and yet her shoulder seemed to almost miss his touch when he turned toward the ditch.

Kali's hormones all but took over her brain, quickly redressing her Knight in Shining Gore-tex in Viking clothes. Then a kilt. And then a slick London suit, just to round off the selection. Yes. They all fit. Every bit as much as his hardy all-weather gear was complementing him now. Maybe he'd just come from an outdoor-clothing catalog shoot.

"Brodie?" Ailsa called to him as he affected a surfing-style skid down the embankment toward the ditch. "She's no patient! This is Kali O'Shea. The new GP."

"Ah."

Brodie came to a standstill, hands shifting up to his hips. His bright blue eyes ricocheted up to Kali, to Ailsa and then back to Kali before he took a decisive step back up the bank.

Kali's eyes widened.

Was he taking back his generous offer?

Abruptly he knelt, grabbed the bike by a single handle and tugged it out of the ditch.

"Here you are, then."

In two long-legged strides he was back atop the embankment, handing over the bike as if it were made out of pond scum…which, now, it kind of was. In two more he was slamming the door to his seen-better-days four-by-four, which he'd parked unceremoniously in the middle of the road.

Brake lights on. Brake lights off.

And with a crunch of gravel and tarmac…away he went.

"Oh, now…" Ailsa sent Kali a mortified look. "That was no way…" She shook her head. "I've never seen him behaving…"

The poor woman didn't seem to be able to form a full sentence. Kali shook her head, to tell her that it didn't matter, nearly choking on a laugh as she did. Her Viking-Fisherman-Calendar Boy's behavior was certainly one way to make an impression! A bit young to be so eccentric, but… welcome to Dunregan!

She shook her head again and grinned. This whole palaver would be a great story to tell when— Well… She was bound to make friends at some juncture. This was her new beginning, and if Mr. Cranky Pants' sole remit was to be eye candy…so be it.

She waved off Ailsa's offer to help, took a hold of the muddy handlebars, and smiled through the spray of mud and scum coming off the spokes as she walked. She was already going to have to change clothes—might as well complete the Ugly Duckling thing she had going on.

"I am *so* sorry. Brodie's not normally so rude," Ailsa apologized.

"Who is he?"

"Don't you know?" Ailsa's eyes widened in dismay.

A nervous jag shot through Kali's belly as she

shook her head. Then the full wattage of real-
ization hit.

"If I were to guess we were going to see him
again at the clinic, would I be right?"

"You'd be right if you guessed you would see
his name beside the clinic door, inside the waiting room and on the main examination room."

"*He's* Dr. McClellan?"

*Terrific! In a really awkward how-on-earth-
is-this-going-to-work? sort of way.*

Kali tried her best to keep her face neutral.

"You'll hear a lot of folk refer to him as *Young*
Dr. McClellan. The practice was originally his father's, but sadly he passed on just recently." Her
lips tightened fractionally. She looked at the expanse of road, as if searching for a bit more of an
explanation, then returned her gaze to Kali with
an apologetic smile. "I'm afraid Brodie's not exactly the roll-out-the-red-carpet type."

Kali couldn't help but smile at the massive understatement.

"More the practical type, eh? Well, that's no
bad thing." Kali was set on finding "the bright
side." Just like the counselor at the shelter had
advised her.

She could hear the woman's words as clearly
as if she'd heard them a moment ago. "It will be
difficult, living without any contact with your
family. But, on the bright side, your life can be
whatever you'd like it to be now."

The words had pinged up in neon in her mental cinema. It was a near replica of the final words her mother had said to her before she'd fled the family home in the middle of the night, five long years ago. Taking a positive perspective had always got her through her darkest days and today would be no different.

"There's only a wee bit to go." Ailsa tipped her head in the direction of an emerging roofline. "Let's get you inside and see if we can't find some dry clothes for you and a hot cup of tea."

Tea!

Bright side.

Brodie had half a mind to drive straight past the clinic and up into the mountains to try to hunt down his brother. Burn off some energy Callum-style on a mountain bike. He was overdue a catch-up since he'd returned. And it wasn't as if he'd be seeing any patients today anyway.

She would.

The new girl.

He tipped his head back and forth. Better get his facts straight.

The new *woman.*

From the looks of Dr. O'Shea, she was no born-and-bred Scottish lassie, that was for sure. Ebony black hair. Long. *Really* long. His fingers involuntarily twitched at the teasing notion of running them through the long, silken swathe. He curled them into a fist and shot his fingers out wide, as if to flick off the pleasurable sensation.

There was more than a hint of South Asia about her. Maybe… Her eyes were a startling light green, and with a surname like O'Shea it was unlikely both of her parents had been Indian born and bred. He snorted. Here he was, angry at the world for making assumptions about him, and he was doing the same thing for poor ol' Kali O'Shea.

When he'd received the email stating a Dr. O'Shea was on her way up he had fully been expecting a red-headed, freckle-faced upstart. Instead she was strikingly beautiful, if not a little wind tousled, like a porcelain doll. With the first light-up-a-room smile he'd seen since he didn't know how long. Not to mention kitted out in entirely inappropriate clothing, riding a ridiculous bicycle on the rough lane and about to begin to do a job he could ruddy well do on his own, thank you very much.

He slowed the car and tugged the steering wheel around in an arc. He'd park behind the building. Leave Kali and Ailsa guessing for a minute. Or ten, given the strength of the gusts they were battling. Why did people insist on riding bicycles in this sort of weather? Ridiculous.

He took his bad mood out on the gear lever, yanking the vehicle into Park and climbing out of the high cab all in one movement.

When his feet landed solidly on the ground it was all too easy to hear his father's voice sounding through his conscience.

You just left her? You left the poor wee thing there on the side of the road, splattered in mud, bicycle covered in muck, and didn't lend a hand? Oh, son... That's not what we islanders are about.

We islanders... Ha! That'd be about right.

And of course his father, the most stalwart of moral compasses, was right. It *wasn't* what Dunreganers were about.

He scrubbed at his hair—a shocker of a reminder that he was long due for a trip to the barber's. He tipped his head up to the stormy skies and barked out a laugh. At least he was free to run his hand through his hair now. And scrub the sleep out of his eyes. Rest his fingers on his lips when in thought...

Not that he'd done much of that lately. A moment's reflection churned up too many images. Things he could never un-see. So it was little wonder his hair was too long, his house was a mess and his life was a shambles ever since he'd returned from Africa. The only thing he was sure of was his status on the island. He'd shot straight up to number one scourge faster than a granny would offer her little 'uns some shortbread.

He slammed his car door shut and dug into his pocket for the practice keys, a fresh wash of rain announcing itself to the already-blustery morning. The one Ailsa and Dr. O'Shea were still battling against.

Fine. All right. He'd been a class-A jerk.

To put it mildly.

He'd put the kettle on. A peace offering to his replacement. *Temporary* replacement, if he could ever convince the islanders that he wasn't contagious. Never had been.

Trust the people who'd known him from the first day he'd taken a breath on this bleak pile of rocks and earth not to believe in the medical clearance he'd received. A clearance he'd received just in time to be at his father's bedside, where they'd been able to make their peace. That was where the first hit of reality had been drilled home. And then there had been the funeral. It was hard to shake off those memories just a fortnight on.

His brother—the stayer—had received the true warmth of the village. Deep embraces. Claps to the shoulder and shared laughter over a fond memory. Only a very few people had shaken hands with him. Everyone else…? Curt nods and a swift exit.

He blamed it on his time in Africa, but his heart told him different. No amount of time would bring back his mother from that sailing trip he'd insisted on taking. No amount of penance would give the island back its brightest rose.

He had thought of giving a talk in the village

hall—about Africa, the medicine he'd practiced, the safety precautions he'd taken—but couldn't bear the thought of standing there on his own, waiting for no one to show up, feeling more of an outsider than he had growing up here.

He shoved the old-fashioned key into the clinic's thick wooden door and pushed the bottom right-hand corner with his foot, where it always stuck when the weather was more wet than cold.

The familiarity of it parted his lips in a grudging smile. He knew this building like the back of his hand. Had all but grown up in it. He'd listened to his first heartbeat here, under the watchful eye of his father. Just as he had done most of his firsts on the island. Beneath his father's ever benevolent and watchful eye.

And now, like his father and his father before him, he was taking over the village practice in a place he knew well. *Too* well. He grimaced as the wind helped give the door a final nudge toward opening.

Without looking behind him he tried to shut it and met resistance. He pushed harder. The door pushed back.

"You're certainly choosing an interesting way to welcome our new GP, Brodie."

Ailsa was behind him, trying to keep the door open for herself and—yes, there she was…just behind Ailsa's shoulder—Dr. Shea.

Dr. *O*'Shea?

Whatever. With the mood he was battling, he was afraid she'd need the luck of the Irish and all of…whatever other heritage it was that he was gleaning.

"Hi, there. I'm Kali." She stepped out from behind Ailsa and put out a scraped hand.

He looked at it and frowned. Another reminder that he should've stuck around to help.

She retracted her hand and wiped it on her mud-stained coat.

"Sorry," she apologized in a soft English accent. One with a lilt. Ireland? It wasn't posh London. "I'm not really looking my best this morning."

"No. Well…"

Brodie gave himself an eye roll. Was it too late to club himself in the forehead and just be done with it?

"Ach, Brodie McClellan! Will you let the poor girl inside so we can get something dry onto her and something hot inside of her?" Ailsa scolded. "Mrs. Glenn dropped some homemade biscuits in yesterday afternoon, when she was out with her dogs. See if you can dig those up while I try and find Dr. O'Shea a towel for all that lovely long hair of hers. And have a scrounge round for some dry clothes, will you?"

"Anything else I can do for you?" he called after the retreating figure, then remembered there was still another woman waiting. One not brave enough to shove past him as Ailsa had. "C'mon, then. Let's get you out of this weather."

Kali eyed Brodie warily as he stepped to the side with an actual smile, his arm sweeping along the hallway in the manner of a charming butler. Hey, presto! And...the White Knight was back in the room. Sort of. His blue eyes were still trained on the car park behind her, as if the trick had really been to make her disappear.

Kali quirked a curious eyebrow as she passed him. Not exactly Prince Charming, was he? *But, my goodness me, he smells delicious.* All sea-peaty and freshly baked bread. With butter. A bit of earthiness was in there, too. An islander. And she was on his turf.

She hid a smile as she envisioned herself helming a Viking invasion ship, a thick fur stole shifting across her shoulders as she pointed out to her crew that she saw land. A raven-haired Vikingess!

Unable to stop the vision, she mouthed, *Land-ho!* with a grin.

Oops! Her eyes flicked to Brodie's. His gaze was still trained elsewhere. Probably just as well.

She looked down the long corridor. A raft of closed doors and not much of a clue as to what was behind them.

"Um...where should I be heading?"

"Down the hall and to your left. First door on

your right once you turn. You'll find Ailsa there in the supplies cupboard."

Brodie closed the outside door and rubbed his hands together briskly, his body taut with energy, as if someone had just changed his batteries.

He had a lovely voice. All rich and rolling *r*'s and broguey. If he weren't so cantankerous… She tilted her head to take another look. Solid jawline, arrestingly blue eyes bright with drive, thick hair a girl could be tempted to run her fingers through.

Yup! Brodie McClellan ticked a lot of boxes. He might be a grump, but he didn't strike her as someone cruel. In fact he seemed rather genuine behind the abruptness.

She envied him that. A man who, in a split second, came across as true to himself. Honest. Even if that honesty *was* as scratchy as sandpaper. Her eyes slid down his arms to his hands. Long, capable fingers, none of which sported a ring. *Huh*… A lone wolf with no designs on joining a pack.

She shook her head, suddenly aware that the lone wolf was speaking to her, though his eyes were trained on his watch.

"So…you'll want to get a move on. I'll just put the kettle on and see you in a couple of minutes so I can talk you through everything, all right? Doors open soon."

He turned into a nearby doorway without further ado. Seconds later Kali could hear a tap running and the familiar sound of a kettle being filled.

Note to self, she thought as her lips twitched into yet another smile, *civilities are a bit different up here.*

None of the normal *How do you do? I'm Dr. fill-in-the-blank, welcome to our clinic. Here's the tea, here's the kettle, put your name on your lunch if you're brave enough to use the staff refrigerator, and we hope you enjoy your time with us, blah-de-blah-de-blah.*

Dr. Brodie McClellan's greeting was the sort of brusque behavior she'd expect in an over-taxed big-city hospital. But here in itsy-bitsy Dunregan, when the clinic wasn't even set to open for another…she glanced at her waterlogged watch… half hour or so… Perhaps he *wasn't* too young to be eccentric. She was going to go with her original assessment. Too honest a human to bother with bog standard social niceties. Even though social niceties were…*nice.*

A clatter of mugs on a countertop broke the silence, followed by some baritone mutterings she couldn't make out.

Well, so what if her new colleague wasn't tuning up the marching band to trill her merrily into her first shift? She'd faced higher hurdles than winning over someone who had obviously flunked out of Charm Academy.

Kali leaned against the wall for a minute. Just to breathe. Realign her emotional bearings. She closed her eyes to see if she could picture the letter inviting her to come to Dunregan. She'd been so ridiculously happy when it had arrived. With so much time "at sea" it had been a moment of pure, unadulterated elation. When the image of the letter refused to come, she pulled her phone out of her pocket so she could pull it up from her emails.

The screen was cracked. Shattered, more like it.

Of course it is! shouted the voice in her head. *It's the least you deserve after what you've done. The trouble you've caused your mother. Your little sister.*

She pressed her hands to her ears, as if that would help silence the voice she fought and fought to suppress on a daily basis.

She huffed a sigh across her lips and looked up to the ceiling. Way up, past the beams, the tiled roofing and the abundance of storm clouds was a beautiful blue sky. And this…? This rocky, discombobulated start was one of those things-could-only-get-better moments. It *had* to be. This was her shot at a completely fresh start. As far away from her father's incandescent rage as she could be.

"Kali, are you—" Ailsa burst into the corridor. "Darlin', did Brodie just leave you standing here in your wet clothes? For heaven's sake. You would've thought the man had been raised by wolves!"

An eruption of colorful language burst forth from the kitchen as Kali eyed the long-sleeved T-shirt from a three-years-old charity run. That and a pair of men's faded track pants were all Ailsa had managed to rustle up.

"Brodie's," Ailsa had informed her.

Her first instinct had been to refuse, but needs must and all that...

Kali stopped for a moment as the soft cotton slid past her nose and she inhaled a hint of washing powder and peat. A web of mixed feelings swept through her as the T-shirt slipped into place boyfriend-style. Over-sized and offering a hint of sexy and secure all at once. She shook her head at her dreamy-eyed reflection in the small driftwood-framed mirror.

It's a shirt! Get over it.

"When are we going to get this blasted kettle fixed?"

Blimey. Had the walls just vibrated?

"Cool your jets, Brodie. For heaven's sake, it's not rocket science. You *do* know how to make a cup of tea, don't you?"

Ailsa's voice whooshed past the bathroom

as she went on her way to the kitchen, her tone soothing as the clink and clatter of mugs and spoons filled out the rest of the mental image Kali was building.

"Stop your fussing, will you?" Brodie grumbled through the stone walls.

"Let *me* have a look," Ailsa chided, much to Kali's amusement. Then, after a moment, "I'll need to get some dressing on that, Dr. McClellan."

"Oh, it's Dr. McClellan now I'm injured, is it?"

"Brodie. Dr. McClellan. You're still the wee boy whose nappies I changed afore you jumped up on my knee, begging me to read you stories about faeries and cowboys over and over, so hush!"

Kali's smile widened as the bickering continued.

Local Doctor Defied by Feisty Kettle:
Nurse Forced to Mollify GP with Bedtime
Stories.

Was that the type of story the local newspaper would run? The population on Dunregan wasn't much bigger than some two thousand or so people, and if memory served she was pretty sure that number accounted for the population surge over the summer months. The *hospitable* months.

"For heaven's sake, Ailsa! Stop your mithering. I don't need a bandage! It's not really even a burn!"

"Well, that's a fine way to treat your head nurse, who has twenty years experience on *you*, Brodie McClellan!"

Kali chalked one up to Ailsa.

"But it's a perfectly normal way to treat my auntie who won't leave well enough alone!"

Brodie's grumpy riposte vibrated through the wall. Kali was relieved to hear Ailsa laugh at her nephew's words, then jumped not a moment later when a door slammed farther along the corridor. *Crikey.* It was like being in a Scottish soap opera. And it was great! No-holds-barred bickering, banter and underneath it all a wealth of love. The stuff of dreams.

Her family had never had that sort of banter—*Stop-stop-stop-stop-stop.* Kali deftly trained her hair into a thick plait as she reminded herself she had no family. No one to bicker with, let alone rely on. Not anymore.

Turn it into a positive, Kali.

The other voice in her head—the kind one, the one that had brought her out of her darkest moments—came through like the pure notes of a flute.

There's always *a bright side.*

Good. Focus on that. Turn it into a positive...

Not having a family means I'm free! Unencumbered! Not a soul in the world to care about me!

The familiar gaping chasm of fear began to tickle at Kali's every confidence.

Okay. Maybe a positive mantra was going to be elusive. For today. But she *could* do it. Eventually. And realistically there was only one mantra she really needed to focus on:

K.I.C.K.A.S.S. Keep It Compassionate, Kind and Supremely Simple.

It had kept her sane for the past five years and would continue to be her theme song.

She tightened the drawstring on the baggy pants and gave her shoulders a fortifying shake. Who knew? Maybe she could get someone with bagpipes to rustle up a tune!

The piper's "K.I.C.K.A.S.S. Anthem."

Hmm. It needed work.

Regardless, the rhythm of the words sang to her in their own way. They were her link to sanity.

She jumped as a door slammed again. Hearing no footsteps, she thought she might as well suck it up and see what was going on out there. No point hiding out in the toilet! In less than thirty minutes she'd be seeing a patient, and it would probably be a good idea to get the lie of the land.

Kali cracked the door open and stuck her head out—only to pull it right back in when Brodie unexpectedly stormed past. If he'd had a riding cloak and a doublet on he would have looked just like the handsome hero from a classic romance.

Handsome?

She was really going to have to stop seeing him in that way. Rude and curt was more like it. And maybe just a little bit sexy Viking.

He abruptly turned and screeched to a halt, one hand holding the other as if in prayer, his index fingers resting upon his lips. His awfully nice lips.

Stop it! You are not to get all mushy about your new boss. Your new, very grumpy boss. You've been down that road and had to leave everything behind. Never again.

She stood stock-still as Brodie's eyes scanned her from top to toe. A little shudder shivered its way along her spine. His gaze felt surprisingly... intimate.

"That's one hell of a look, Dr. O'Shea."

As Brodie's blue eyes worked their way along her scrappy ensemble for a second time Kali all but withered with embarrassment. Snappy comebacks weren't her forte. Not by a long shot.

"Once I get a lab coat on it should be all right."

Nice one, Kali.

"Sure." Brodie turned and resumed his journey to the front of the clinic. "I'll just get the patient list."

Kali did a skip-run-walk thing to catch up with his long-legged strides.

"Would you like me to take a look?"

"That's generally the idea with a patient list."

Kali blew out a slow breath, her eyes on Brodie's retreating back as she continued race-walking to keep up with him. Touchy, touchy! She was next to certain he wasn't angry with *her*, but there was a bagpipe-sized chip on that shoulder of his.

"I meant your hand."

Brodie stopped short and whirled around. Kali only just skidded to a halt in time not to run into his chest. Which, given how nice he smelled, wouldn't have been too bad a thing, but—

"I'd have thought you'd be too afraid."

"Wh-what?" Kali instinctively pulled back at Brodie's aggressive response. She'd been afraid before. Terrified, actually. For her life. And she'd survived.

She pressed her heels into the ground. If she could make a last-minute exit out of an arranged marriage under the threat of death she could deal with a grumpy thirtysomething doctor with a self-induced kettle burn.

"I've dealt with difficult patients before," she continued levelly, her eyes on his hand. Meeting his gaze would only increase the heated atmosphere. "I'm sure we'll come out all right in the end."

"Difficult patients with Ebola?"

Brodie thrust his hand forward and with every pore of strength she could muster Kali held her ground. She had no idea what he was talking about, but she was not—absolutely, positively *not*—going to start out her new life fearfully.

"Aren't you going to touch it?"

He thrust his hand straight into her eyeline— millimeters from her face. What *was* this? Some sort of hardcore newcomer test? Whatever it was, she was not going to be frightened by Brodie McClellan or anyone—ever again.

Brodie watched, amazed, as Kali stood stock-still, seemingly unfazed by his ridiculously aggressive behavior. She took his hand in hers, one of her delicate fingers holding open his own as they instinctively tried to curl round the injury. It was the first time he'd been touched by someone outside of a medical exam in weeks, if not months. The power of it struck him deeply.

Kali's delicate touch nearly released the soft moan building in his chest. He couldn't— *mustn't*—let her see how much this single moment meant to him. He looked at her eyes as they moved across his hand. Diligent, studied. Their extraordinary bright green making them almost feline. More tigress than tabby, he thought.

Moments later, as he exhaled, he realized he'd been holding his breath while Kali was examining him with clinical indifference—examining the burn mark he'd all but shoved directly in her face. It wasn't a bad burn. His pride had been hurt more than his hand. Her touch had been more healing than any medicine. Not that he'd ever tell her. She'd be off soon. Like all the good things that came into his life. Just passing through.

Her long lashes flicked up over those green eyes of hers meeting his inquisitive gaze head-on. Could she see how strange this was for him? Being treated as if he *weren't* a walking, talking contagious disease? No. It ran deeper than that. She was treating him compassionately. Without the stains of his past woven through her understanding of who he actually was.

"That's all you've got?"

"I'm sorry?" Brodie near enough choked at her about-face, bring-it-on attitude.

"Ebola?" She scoffed. "That's your best shot?"

Now it was Brodie's turn to be confused. Was she trying to double bluff him?

"I get a bit of hazing, Dr. McClellan. The less than warm welcome, the mocking about this ridiculous outfit. But seriously...?" She snorted a *get real* snort, took a step back, her hand still holding his, and gave him a smile wreathed in skepticism. "That's your best shot at getting me to hightail it back to the mainland, is it? Ebola?"

CHAPTER TWO

BRODIE PULLED HIS hand out of Kali's and received an indignant stare in response.

"What? Now I'm not fit to see to a first-degree burn? I am a qualified GP, I'll have you know."

This time there was fire behind her words. *She was no pushover.* He liked that. Decorum ruled all here on Dunregan and it had never been a good fit for him. It was what had forced him to head out into the world to explore who he could be without That Day branded onto his every move.

Enough with the bitterness, McClellan. You're not a teenager anymore.

"No, that's not it at all." Brodie waved away her presumption, opting to get over himself and just be honest. "I think the booking agency might not have been entirely forthright with you."

"What are you talking about? Four weeks—with the possibility of an extension. What's there to know beyond that?" Her forehead crinkled ever so slightly.

"I…" Brodie hesitated, then plunged forward. No point in beating round the bush. "I've recently finished my twenty-one-day clearance after three months working in an Ebola hospital. In Africa," he added, as if it weren't ruddy obvious where the hospital had been.

Three countries. Thousands dead. He'd wanted to make a difference. Needed to make a difference somewhere—*anywhere*—before coming back here. And he had done. Small-scale. But he'd been there. A pair of hazmat boots on the ground in a place where "risky" meant that sharing the same air as the person next to you might mean death. Only to come back and face a sea of incriminating looks.

Is this what you had in mind, Dad? Making me promise to work on the island for a year after you'd gone so I could be reminded how much of an outsider I am?

He shook off the thought. His father had been neither bitter nor vengeful. It had been his fathomless kindness and understanding that had driven the stakes of guilt deep into Brodie's heart.

"Hmm…"

Kali's green-eyed gaze remained steady apart from a blink or two. Could she see the inner turmoil he was fighting? Filial loyalty over a need to cut loose? To forge his own path.

Kali's voice, when she finally spoke, was completely neutral. "Guess they *did* leave that bit out." She considered him for a moment longer. "I am presuming you wouldn't be here if you hadn't had the all clear so…it does beg the question: what am I doing here if you're good to go?"

"Ah, the mysteries of life in Dunregan begin to reveal themselves." This was the part that rankled. The part where Brodie found himself slamming doors, spilling boiling water and leaving unsuspecting GPs with their muck-covered bicycles by the side of the road on a stormy day.

"Some of—*most* of the patients are *concerned*…about being seen by me." Total honesty? *All* of them. Fear of catching Ebola from Ol' Dr. McClellan's son had gripped the island.

Or…the thought struck him…maybe they had simply preferred his father and were using the Ebola scare as an excuse to refuse his treatment. Now, *that* hurt.

He cleared his throat. One step at a time.

"Even though you've had the all clear?" Kali's voice remained impartial. She was fact gathering.

"Right. Apparently most folk round here don't put much faith in the Public Health Office's green light." He snorted derisively. "And to think of all the viral infections I've treated here. Rich, isn't it?"

He stopped himself. He was going to have to check the bitter tone in his voice. Yeah, he was angry. But he was hurting much more than he was spitting flames. And to add on moments like these—moments that reminded him why he wanted more than anything to live somewhere else. Oh, to be anonymous!

"I'm going to presume, as someone who has

also taken the Hippocratic oath, that you wouldn't have returned to your practice until you felt well and truly able to."

Despite himself, he shot her a look. One that said, *Obviously not. Otherwise I wouldn't be so blinking frustrated.*

"Don't shoot the messenger, Dr. McClellan! I wouldn't be doing my job if I didn't check with you."

"Fair enough."

And it was. It just felt…*invasive*…being questioned again. And by someone who hadn't been through the post-Ebola wringer as he had.

Kali might be a fully qualified GP, but her face was unlined by personal history. With skin that smooth, no dark circles under her eyes, excited to be working in *Dunregan*… She had to be green around the ears.

"What are you? Two…three days out of med school?"

She looked at him as if he'd sprouted horns. The rod of steel reasserted itself.

"Old enough. Apart from which, I don't really think that's any business of yours."

"No." Might as well be honest. "You just look—"

"Yeah, yeah. I know." She all but spat the words out, crossing her arms defensively across her chest. "Baby-faced."

"Not exactly what I was going to say," Brodie

countered. *Arrestingly beautiful* would've been more accurate. Her smooth skin was entirely un-weathered by life, but now that he was paying more attention the wary look in her eyes spoke of wisdom beyond her years.

"Well…" She adopted a tone one might use for toddlers. "I'm a fully fledged grown-up, just like you, so you can rest easy, Dr. McClellan."

"Brodie," he countered with a smile.

He was warming to Kali. The more they spoke the more it seemed they might be two of a kind. Quick to smart when someone hit the right buttons. Slow to trust. A well-earned friendship if you ever got that far.

"Well, guess you're just lucky. Good genes from your parents, eh?"

She stiffened.

More sensitive territory, from the looks of things. Maybe her relationship with *her* family was as terrific as the one he had with his. One wayward brother, a meddling auntie and a god-send of a niece who'd stepped in at the reception desk when his "loyal" long-term sidekick had flown the coop. Okay…so they weren't that bad. But right now he was feeling a bit more me-against-the-world than he liked.

"So…you were working in Africa…?"

Score one to Kali for deftly changing the topic!

"Right, sorry." Brodie regrouped with a shake of his head. "Okay—long story short: I did the work through Doctors Without Borders who—as I'm sure you will appreciate—have some pretty rigorous safety systems in place for this sort of thing. I was lucky enough to be working in one of the newly built facilities. Upon my return to the UK…" he glanced at the date on his phone "…which was about five weeks ago, I went to a pre-identified debriefing under the watchful eye of Public Health England."

"PHE? I know it." Kali nodded for him to continue before noticing Ailsa coming down the corridor, her arms laden with patient files.

"Oh, Dr. O'Shea! Glad to see you in some dry clothes. If you'd just like to hang yours on the radiator in the tea room at the back there—where we came in—they should be dry in no time. I'll see about finding you a white coat as well, but folk don't stand too much on formality here. What you have on now will do just fine."

Ailsa squeezed between the pair of them on her way to her office, giving Brodie a bit of a glare as she did. He gave her a toothy grin in return. He knew he was a pain in the bum, but that was what number one nephews were for!

Ailsa Dunregan was a brilliant nurse. And a vigilant auntie. It meant more than he could say that she hadn't fled the coop like the rest of his staff. Well, the receptionist. Best not get too hysterical.

He returned his focus to Kali. All gamine and sexy looking in his castoffs. Who knew a scrubby T-shirt and joggers could look so...rip-offable?

He gave his head a quick shake. Kali was showing professionalism. Now it was his turn.

"Okay, the clinic is going to be opening soon so—in a nutshell—there's a twenty-one-day incubation period. I stayed near a PHE-approved facility and did the following: I took my temperature twice a day, called my 'fever parole officer,' did a full course of malaria prophylaxis, because malaria symptoms can mimic Ebola symptoms. Any hint of a fever and I was meant to isolate myself and call the paramedics—like that doctor in New York. Who also got the all clear, by the way," he added hastily.

"Where did you do all this?" Kali asked.

"I stayed in London so that I was near an appropriate treatment center should any of the symptoms have arisen, and I spoke regularly with hospital staff just to triple-check everything I was experiencing was normal."

She quirked an eyebrow.

"It makes you paranoid. Hemorrhagic fever ain't pretty." He checked his tone. Kali hadn't said a word of judgment. She wasn't the enemy. Just a GP doing her job. *His* job. Whatever.

He started over. "Three months in protective gear, vigilant disinfections and then nothing. I'd never realized how often people sneeze on public transport before." He tried for a nonchalant chortle and ended up coughing. *Sexy.* Not that he was trying to appeal to Kali on any level other than as a doctor or anything.

"Right." Kali took back the conversation's reins before his thoughts went in too wayward a direction. "I take it you've spoken with everyone? The islanders?" she clarified.

He swallowed. *Not in so many words...*

Kali watched Brodie's Adam's apple dip and surge, her eyes flicking up to his in time to see his gaze shift up to the right. So *that* was his tell.

She was hoping he hadn't felt her fingers shaking earlier when she had held his palm in hers. Countless self-defense courses hadn't knocked the infinitesimal tremor out of her hands. But when Brodie had thrown the Ebola grenade into her lap years of medical training and logic had dictated that she'd be fine. Instinctually she knew that she had a jacked-up instinct for survival. It had never come to that, but if she needed to fight for her life she had the skills to give it her all.

"Depends upon what you mean, exactly...by 'spoken with.'" Brodie's gaze returned to hers, his fingers dropping some air quotes into the space between them. As their eyes met—his such a clear blue—she wondered that anyone could doubt him. They were the most honest pair of eyes she had ever seen. She felt an unexpected hit of disappointment that she wouldn't be here in Dunregan longer than a few weeks.

She shook her head, reminding herself they were in the middle of a pretty important conversation.

"So, you've not held a town hall meeting or anything like that?"

Just the look on his face was enough to tell her he hadn't.

"Maybe you've had an article in the...what's the local paper?"

"The *Dunregan Chronicle*."

"I'm asking, not telling," she reminded him when his tone lurched from informational to confrontational. "Have you had anything published? An article? An interview?"

"No, I've been a bit busy burying my father, amongst other things," Brodie snapped, instantly regretting it.

Quit shooting the messenger, idiot!

He gave Kali an apologetic glance. "I thought the ever-reliable gossip circuit on the island would cover all of my bases. Which it did. Just not in the way I'd thought."

"Look. If it's all right, I'm going to stop you there," Kali jumped in apologetically. "I'm really sorry to hear about your father. Now—not that the nuts and bolts of how this island works aren't interesting—I really need to get a handle on how things work right here." Kali flicked her thumb toward the front of the clinic. "If you're happy to meet me after the clinic's shut I'd love to hear all about it. Your work in Africa," she qualified quickly. "It sounds fascinating."

"It was an unbelievable experience. I'll never forget it."

Wow! The first person who'd actually seemed interested!

"So…" She gave her shoulders a wriggle, as if to regroup.

A wriggle inside *his* shirt, with more than a hint of shoulder slipping in and then out of the stretched neckline. A tug of attraction sent his thoughts careening off to a whole other part of his—er—brain? Another time, another place?

Focus, man! The poor woman's trying to speak with you.

"If I was in your shoes I wouldn't want me here either. It's *your* practice! But I'm here to help, not hinder."

He nodded. Wise beyond her years. Those green eyes of her held untold stories. He'd been wrong to think otherwise.

"Can we shake on it?" She thrust her hand forward, chin jutted upwards. Not in defiance, more in anticipation of a problem.

He put his hand forward—the one he hadn't burned—for a sound one-two shake.

"Are we good?"

"Yes, ma'am?" He affected an American accent and gave her a jaunty salute.

Her eyes narrowed a bit.

Okay, fine. He blew that one.

"We're good. I'll steer clear of tea duty."

She furrowed her brow at him in response.

Quit being such a jerk. Like she said, she's here to help!

She shifted past him in the corridor, leaving the slightest hint of jasmine in her wake. "I should probably go introduce myself up front."

"Yes—yeah. On you go. Caitlyn's my niece and is about as much of a newcomer to the clinic as you are."

"Excellent." Kali gave him a polite smile. "She and I can forge into unknown territory together, then. And don't worry about the tea. I'm more of a coffee girl."

Her tone was bright, non-confrontational.

"We've not given you much of a welcome, have we?"

Kali rocked back on her heels with a squelch, not looking entirely sure how to respond until she saw the edges of Brodie's lips tweak up into a slow but generous grin.

"Ailsa's great!" Kali shot back with her own cheeky grin. Adding, "I've yet to make a decision on the boss man…"

"He's a real piece of work." Brodie was laughing now. "But he's good at his job."

"I don't doubt that for a minute."

And he could see she meant it. He *was* a good doctor. A little shy on bedside manner, but—

"Oh, and as for that hand of yours—you probably don't need a bandage, but it might be a good idea to put some topical sulfonamide antibacterial cream on there. Although, as you probably know, some new studies suggest it might actually lengthen the healing time."

Brodie gave a grin as Kali shrugged off her own advice before tacking on, "I'm sure you know what's best, Old Timer..." as she pushed through the swinging door into the front of the clinic.

Kali gave as good as she got. Just as well, given his zigzagging moods.

Brodie put his hand to the door to talk Caitlyn and Kali through their intro but stopped at his aunt's less than subtle clearing of her throat.

"And what can I help you with on this fine day, my dear Auntie?"

"You're not thinking of going in there and looming over Caitlyn, are you?"

"No."

Yes.

"Give the girl a chance. She's only just out of school and she doesn't need her uncle hovering over her every step of the way."

"What? Do you think I might accidentally

breathe too much in the reception area and frighten away even more patients?"

"Brodie McClellan." Ailsa wagged a finger at him. "You'd best think twice about pushing so hard against the support system you have. Caitlyn's here until she starts university in September—but after that… Only a few months for you to make your peace with everyone. Including…" she steeled her gaze at him "…Dr. O'Shea. She's here to *help*, might I remind you?"

"Help for something that's not actually a problem?"

"You know what I mean, Brodie. C'mon." She gave his shoulder a consoling rub. "You can't blame folk for being nervous. And besides, you're only fresh back. It'll give you time to settle back in. Mend a couple of fences while you're at it."

She gave him her oft-used Auntie Knows Best stare.

He could do as she suggested. Of course he could. Or he could go back home and pack his bag and head back on another Doctors Without Borders assignment until Kali was gone.

A hit of protectiveness for his father's surgery took hold.

Unexpected.

Or was it curiosity about Kali?

Interesting.

He leaned against the wall and gave his aunt his best I'll-give-it-a-try face.

"So, after all the miraculous recoveries of the bumper-to-bumper patients we normally have over the past couple of weeks, do you think they'll come flooding back now that we have Kali here?"

"Most likely."

His aunt had never been one to mince words.

"So what am *I* meant to do? Just twiddle my thumbs whilst Kali sees to folk?"

"I suspect she'll need some help. You would be showing her the *good* side of yourself if you were to talk her through a patient's history. Give her backup support if she needed it. Prove to her you're the lovable thirty-two-year-old I've had the pleasure of knowing all my life instead of that fusty old curmudgeon you showed her this morning. I'll tell you, Brodie—I didn't much like seeing that side of you. It's not very fetching."

"Fine." He pressed back from the wall with a foot. "Maybe it'd be best if I just leave well enough alone. Let you two run the show and I'll—I don't know—I'll build that boat I always had a mind to craft."

The words were out before he could stem them.

"You mean the one your father always wanted to build with you?" Ailsa nodded at the memory, completely unfazed by his burst of temper. "That's one promise you could make good on. Or you could put all of that energy you've got winging around inside of you helping out the new doctor who's come all the way up here to get you out of a right sorry old pickle. Then make good on the *other* promise you made to your father."

They both knew what she meant.

"I'm here, aren't I?"

"That's not what I meant, nor your father and you know it, Broderick Andrew McClellan."

Brodie had to hand it to her. Whipping out all three of his names—that was fighting talk for Ailsa.

She pursed her lips at him for added measure, clearly refusing to rise—or lower herself—to his level of self-pity. And frankly he was bored with it himself. He'd never been one for sulky self-indulgence. Or standing around idly doing nothing.

He had twiddling his thumbs down to a fine art now. Not to mention a wind farm's worth of energy to burn. He gave the wall a good thump with the sole of his boot.

Ailsa turned away, tsking as she went back into her office to prepare for the day. Which would most likely be busy now that Kali was here.

"It's not like I was away having the time of my life or anything!" he called after her.

She stuck her head out into the corridor again, but said nothing.

"People were dying in droves!"

"Yes, you were an incredibly compassionate, brave man to go and do what you did—and it's a shame folk here haven't quite caught up with that. But with you looking like you've got the weight of the world on your shoulders it's little wonder you've become so unapproachable."

"Unapproachable! *Me?*" He all but bellowed it, just as Kali walked into the hallway—only to do an immediate about-face back into the reception area.

Ailsa gave him an I-told-you-so look. Brodie took a deep breath in to launch into a well-rehearsed list of the things wrong with Dunregan and her residents, and just as quickly felt the puff go out of him. It would take an hour to rattle off the list of things wrong with *himself* this morning, let alone address the big picture.

For starters he'd been rude to Kali. Unprofessional. Then had thrown a blinkin' tantrum over a burn that had happened solely because he'd been slamming around a kettle of boiling water in a huff because he had to tell yet *another* person why he was toxic.

The word roiled round his gut.

He wasn't *toxic*! He was fit as a fiddle set to play for an all-hours fiddle fest! But he knew more than most it ran deeper than that. How to shrug off the mantle of the tortured laddie who'd sailed out on a handmade skiff with his mum, only to be washed ashore two hours later when the weather had turned horribly, horribly fierce?

He knew it was a miracle he'd survived. But he would've swapped miracles any day of the week if only his mother could have been spared.

"You know, Ailsa…"

His aunt gave him a semi-hopeful look when she heard the change in his tone.

"A second pair of hands round this place would be helpful longer term, wouldn't it? Female hands. You're wonderful—obviously—but Dad always spoke of having a female GP around. Someone not from Dunregan to give the islanders a bit more choice when they need to talk about sensitive issues."

As he spoke the idea set off a series of fireworks in his brain. New possibilities. With Kali on board as a full-time GP he wouldn't have to kill himself with office hours, out-of-hours emergency calls, home visits and the mountain rescues that cropped up more often than not during the summer season.

Not that he minded the work. Hell, he'd work every hour of the day if he could. But working here was much more than ferrying patients in and out for their allotted ten minutes. And if he was going to make good on his deathbed promise to his father to work in the surgery for at least a year he wasn't so sure doing it alone would get the intended results…

His grandfather and his father had prided themselves on being genuine, good-as-their-word *family* doctors. Their time and patience had gone beyond patching up wounds, scribbling out prescriptions and seeing to annual checkups. Here on Dunregan it was personal. Everything was. It was why his father's premature death from cancer had knocked the wind out of the whole population. Everyone knew everyone else and everything about them.

Sharing the load with Kali might be the way he'd get through the year emotionally intact. Maybe even restore some of his tattered reputation. Everyone who'd ever met his father thought the world of him. John McClellan: treasured island GP.

The same could not be said of himself.

Ailsa eyed him warily. "You're not just saying this to get out of the promise to your father, are you?"

"No." He struggled to keep the emotion out of his voice. A bedside promise to a dying father… It didn't get more Shakespearean than that.

"Well, my dear nephew, if you're wanting Dr. O'Shea to stick around you best check she's not already legged it out the front of the clinic. You need to show her the other side of Brodie McClellan. The one we all like."

She gave his cheek a good pinch. Half loving, half scolding.

He laughed and pulled her into her arms for a hug.

"What would I do without you and your wise old ways, Auntie Ailsa? I've been a right old pill this morning, haven't I?"

"I'm hardly old, and there are quite a few ways I could describe your behavior, Brodie—but your way is the most polite." Ailsa's muffled voice came from his chest. "Now…" She pushed back and looked him square in the eye. "Let me get on with my day, will you?"

As she disappeared into her office so, too, did the smile playing across his lips. Here he was, blaming the islanders for the situation he was in, when truthfully all his frustration came from the fact that he loved his father and his work and right now the two were at odds. Not one part of him was looking forward to the year ahead.

Truthfully? He needed Kali O'Shea more than he cared to admit. If he could convince her to stay she might be the answer to all his prayers. A comrade in arms to help him get through the thicket of weeds he was all but drowning in.

He jogged his shoulders up and down.

Right. Good.

Time for what his father had called a "Starty-Overy, I've Done A Whoopsy." His behavior this morning had been childish. He might as well give it the childish name. Then start acting his age and focus on winning over the mysteriously enigmatic Dr. Kali O'Shea.

Kali tapped at her computer keyboard a second time. Then pressed Refresh. And again.

Weird.

There didn't seem to be anyone next in the queue. She stuck her head round the corner into the office where Brodie had been lurking... Okay, not exactly lurking. He'd been "on hand" in case she needed any information. But it had felt like lurking.

"Hey, does the computer system get jammed sometimes?"

"All the time is more like it," he answered with a smile.

Her stomach grumbled. Kali's hand flew to cover it, as if it would erase the fact it had happened.

"Er..."

"Hungry after only seeing three patients?" Brodie teased.

"Something like that. I was too excited for my first day at work to eat breakfast."

"Only fifteen more patients to go before lunch!"

"Or..." She drew out the word and thought she might as well push her luck. "I do seem to recall an offer of a cup of tea and a biscuit."

He blinked, dragging a tooth across one of those full lips of his. Distracting. *Very* distracting.

"Would you like it if I put on a pinny and pushed a wee cart along to your office for delivery, Dr. O'Shea?"

A flush of embarrassment crept up her cheeks.

He was an experienced doctor. Her superior. Had she pushed that envelope too far?

"Ach, take that nervous expression off your face, Dr. O'Shea. I'm just joshing you." He stood up from his desk and gave her shoulder a squeeze. "A nice cup of tea is the least I can do an hour after I promised it."

He dropped her a wink and her tummy did a flip. The sexy kind.

Oh, no. Not good. Not good at all.

"Right, well…I guess I better check with Caitlyn who's next." She gave the door frame a rap, as if that was the signal for action. Then didn't move.

"Anything good this morning?"

"Depends upon your definition of 'good,'" she replied with a smile. She liked this guy. He was a whole load nicer than Dr. McCrabby from this morning. "A prenatal check, a suspected case of the flu—which thankfully wasn't more than a really bad cold—and a check on a set of stitches along a feisty four-year-old's hairline. Rosie Bell, I think her name was."

"That's her mother. The daughter is Julia."

"Right—that's right. I mean, of *course* you know it's right—you know everyone." She stopped herself. She was blathering. "The stitches were just fine. She had them put in on the mainland, at the hospital, there…so…that was a quickie. Everyone has been incredibly welcoming…"

So much for no more blathering.

A shadow darkened Brodie's eyes for a moment. He abruptly slipped through the doorway and headed down the hall. "Best go get my pinny on and leave you to it, then, Dr. O'Shea."

"Thank you," she said to his retreating back, wishing the ground had swallowed her up before she'd opened her big mouth.

But it was the truth. Everyone *had* been really welcoming and it felt amazing! Never in her adult life had she been part of a community, and this place seemed to just…*speak* to her.

Her tummy grumbled again.

Dinner.

She would ask Brodie to join her for dinner and then maybe she would stop saying the wrong thing all the time. Fingers crossed and all that.

"Who's next, please, Caitlyn?" Kali stuck her head into the receptionist's room, willing herself onto solid terrain. Seeing patients was the one thing in the world that grounded her. Gave her the drive to find some place where she could settle down and play a positive role in her patients' lives.

"Sorry, Dr. O'Shea… I've been trying to send it through on your computer screen. I've not yet got the hang of the system with all of these patients showing up like this."

Kali peeked beyond Caitlyn and out into the busy waiting room.

"It's not normally like this?"

"Well…" Caitlyn used her feet to wheel herself and her chair over to Kali, lowering her voice to a confidential tone. "Since I started last week it's all been mostly people here to see Auntie Ail—I mean, Sister Dunregan. But most of the people who canceled appointments when Unc—Dr. McClellan came back seem to have all magically turned up now they've heard you arrived…"

"I only got in last night."

"Aye, but you were on the public ferry, weren't you?"

Kali nodded. It was the only way onto the island unless you owned a private helicopter. Which she most assuredly did not.

"Word travels fast round here."

Kali laughed appreciatively as the outside door opened and another person tried to wedge her way onto the long window seat bench after giving Caitlyn a little wave in lieu of checking in.

"Hello, Mrs. Brown. We'll see what we can do, all right? You might have a wee wait," Caitlyn called.

"That's fine, dear. I've brought my knitting."

"So people are just coming along and trying their luck?" Kali's eyes widened.

"Something like that." Caitlyn nodded. "No

harm in trying, is there? Hey!" Her eyes lit up with a new idea. "I bet you'll get in the paper!"

Kali felt a chill jag along her spine and forced herself to smile. "Well, I doubt me being here is *that* big a deal."

"On *this* island? You'd be surprised what turns up in the paper. There was a notice put in when my hamster Reggie died."

She pulled her chair back up to the window that faced the reception area and started tapping at the computer keyboard to pull up the next patient's information.

Kali crossed her fingers behind her back, hoping that her arrival on Dunregan didn't warrant more attention than a full waiting room. *That* she could deal with. Public notice? No. That would never do. So much for unpacking her bags and staying awhile.

"Oh! Dr. O'Shea—I'm such an airhead. Sorry. Would you mind seeing Mr. Alexander Logan first? He's just come in and says it's an emergency. He didn't look all that well…"

"Absolutely." Kali nodded.

Medicine. And keeping her head down. Those were her two points of focus. Time to get on with medicine.

CHAPTER THREE

"ALEXANDER LOGAN?" Kali swung open the door leading into the waiting room.

"Aye, that's me." A gentleman with a thick shock of gray hair tried to press himself up from the bench seat, flat cap in one hand, cane in the other. "And you are…?"

"Dr. O'Shea. I'm the new—the locum doctor."

"With a name like O'Shea and those green eyes of yours I'm guessing you must be Irish." He grinned at her, eyes shining.

Kali hoped he didn't see the wince of pain his question had elicited. He wasn't to know that her mother—her *ballast*—with her distant Irish connection was the only reason she was alive.

"My wife was Irish. Feisty."

Just like her mother.

"She sounds like a great woman," she replied with a smile, grateful to dodge the question about herself. "You all right there, Mr. Logan? Would you like a hand standing up?"

"Oh, no—well, a bit." He looked up at her with a widening smile. "Yes, those eyes of yours remind me of Tilly, all right."

Kali hooked her arm through his, relieved to feel him put a bit of his body weight on her arm.

"Shall we try and work our way to the exam room?"

"Oh, sure. Not as quick on my—" He lifted his hand to his mouth, as if he were waiting for a sneeze to arrive. When the sneeze came, he stumbled forward, losing his grip on his cane as he fell, then let out a howl of pain.

Half the people in the waiting room lurched forward to lend a hand as Kali tightened her grip on his elbow and shifted an arm round his waist.

She heard the swinging door open behind her.

"Sandy?" It was Brodie.

"I'm all right...just me hip."

He was clearly the opposite of all right, but as Brodie stepped forward to help support Mr. Logan Kali could feel the older man press closer to her.

"No, no..." Mr. Logan gave a little wave of his hand. "It's all right, Brodie. I've got Dr. O'Shea here, seeing to me."

Kali was surprised to see fear in the man's eyes. No one in that waiting room looked healthier than Brodie McClellan. The man was a veritable poster boy for the ruggedly fit.

"I was just—" Brodie began, then gave up. "Caitlyn, can you call Ailsa and have her help Mr. Logan into the exam room? I'm guessing your hip is giving you gyp again, Sandy?"

"Aye, well..."

That was all the older man would allow. Kali

couldn't figure out if that was a standard Scottish response or if he was trying to breathe less now that Brodie was in the room. Out of the corner of her eye she saw one of the other patients bring a tissue to her lips. The sea of helping hands had been withdrawn entirely.

She was surprised to realize she was feeling indignant. On Brodie's behalf. She'd known within minutes of meeting him that he wouldn't compromise someone's health...well, maybe in *quite a few* minutes... Even so, the man meant no harm. Quite the opposite, in fact.

"If you two have a history, I'm happy for you to see Dr. McClellan, if you prefer," Kali offered. Might as well try to build bridges out here in the public eye.

"Oh, no dear." Mr. Logan put more of his weight on Kali. "You understand, Brodie—don't you? I wouldn't want to seem rude to Dr. O'Shea, when she's gone to all this trouble to come up here to Dunregan." His eyes flicked between the two doctors. "Would I, Dr. McClellan?"

It was an apology. Not a question.

"Of course not, Mr. Logan." Brodie dropped the informal abbreviation he'd used earlier and grabbed a couple of antiseptic wipes from the counter before bending over to pick up the man's cane. He gave it a visible scrub along the arch as he did.

Kali's eyes flicked to Ailsa as she entered the

room, watching her assess the situation before taking the cane from Brodie with a bright smile. He disappeared into the back of the clinic before Kali could catch his eye. Get a reading on how much the incident had hurt. She would've felt it if it had happened to her, and she didn't even know these people.

"Oh, dearie me, Mr. Logan," chirped Ailsa. "It looks like your new hip isn't quite playing ball, is it?"

"It's been fine, but Bess and I were walking along Ben Regan—"

"Away up on the cliffs?"

"Aye, well… Going up was all right, but the going down part… Well, it's just not felt quite right since then."

"Are you up to the journey down the corridor, Sandy? Any sciatic pain before you went on your walk?"

"No, no. I did that flexing test thing Brodie showed me the last time." He shot a guilty look at the space Brodie had vacated.

"Did you feel the hip come out of the socket?" Kali asked.

"Just now? Aye, that I did."

Ailsa shot Kali a look which she interpreted as, *Are you up to doing a hip relocation?* Kali nodded, her lips pressed grimly together. Mr. Logan wasn't exactly light.

"With the two of you lassies helping me, I

should be fine to get to the room." Mr. Logan gave them each a grateful smile.

Not two or three steps into the corridor he sneezed again and all but crumpled to the floor.

"Well, all right, then, Mr. Logan." Kali nodded at Ailsa as she spoke. "I guess we'll get to it right here, if that's okay."

"Anything…" he huffed out. "Anything to stop the pain."

Kali straightened both of the gentleman's legs out onto the corridor floor—one was visibly shorter than the other—taking a glimpse up to his face as the left knee refused to unbend. The color was fading from Mr. Logan's cheeks and his breath was coming in short, sharp pants.

"Mr. Logan? It looks like you've got a posterior dislocation here. I'm just going to take your leg—"

"Do whatever you need to do quickly, lassie!" Mr. Logan panted.

"Ailsa—Mrs. Dunregan—Nurse—" Kali stumbled over the words—she still wasn't up to name etiquette in this place where everyone knew everyone. "Would you mind holding Mr.—Sandy's head steady?"

"I'd probably be best holding down his pelvic bones for you when you do the reduction," Ailsa corrected gently. "Mr. Logan and I aren't going anywhere. You go on and get whatever medication you need."

"Right." She shot a look over her shoulder, as if some medication would magically appear, then whispered, "I've only ever done this procedure with a patient under general anesthetic in surgery."

"But you've done it?" Ailsa's voice was low.

"Yes, but…"

"We don't have a hospital on Dunregan, dear. Mr. Logan's had a hip replacement, so he's got an artificial ball joint. You'll need to perform a reduction of the dislocated hip prosthesis, okay? Sooner rather than later. You'll be fine," she added with a reassuring smile.

Kali rose and jogged to the exam room she'd been using to find Brodie, hands sheathed in protective gloves, filling a syringe with something.

"Morphine." Brodie pinched the syringe between two fingers, handing it to her with the needle still capped. "And you will probably also want to give him this."

"Which is…?" Kali hoped the panic she was feeling wasn't as obvious as it felt.

"Midazolam. For sedation." He handed her the syringe with a gloved hand. "Are you sure you're good with this?"

"Yes, of course," she answered—too swiftly.

"So you've done a hip relocation in these circumstances?"

Not in the strictest sense of the words.

She looked up at Brodie's face. Was he doubting her or offering reassurance? There was kindness in his eyes. He gave her a *go on* nod.

"I've got it. I'm good." She gave a firm nod in return, convincing herself as much as Brodie. This was just another one of those moments when life wasn't giving her much of a choice. Her patient had specifically requested her as his doctor, and it seemed Brodie was in her corner.

"Any special tips for Mr. Logan's hip?" She hoped the question wasn't a giveaway that her brain was short-circuiting.

"Nope."

Brodie turned back to the sink to peel off his gloves and wash his hands. Or to ignore her.

Both?

So much for being in her corner! She stared at his back, tempted, just for a moment, to stick out her tongue at him. She wasn't *that* long out of med school and, whilst she *had* done a reduction before, she certainly hadn't done one under these circumstances.

Well, tough. That was what she had and she would just have to cope.

"Are you going to do the reduction or do you need help?" Brodie didn't turn around, his question rising only slightly above the sound of running water. It was difficult to tell if his tone was kind or frustrated.

"It's not as if there's anyone else we can ring, is

there?" Kali asked rhetorically, instantly wishing she hadn't when his shoulders stiffened.

Open mouth…insert foot. The poor man's father wasn't long gone and he was having just about the worst period of mourning a son could go through. He had her compassion.

"I'm good. I've got it." She spoke to his back again, shook herself into action and took a careful look at each of the syringes she held. Brodie had labeled them.

A tray appeared in her eyeline, preset with alcohol prep pads, tape and a blunt-end needle already attached to a high-flow extension tube with a four-way stopcock. Her eyes flicked up and she gave Brodie a grateful smile. His neutral expression gave nothing away—but his actions were clear. The man was meticulous. And his patient's welfare was paramount. Otherwise he wouldn't be here—hovering, checking she was up to snuff. Which she'd better get busy proving she was.

"Thanks for doing the syringes. And the tray. Everything."

She didn't catch his mumbled reply as she picked up her pace to get back to her patient.

"You'll need these as well."

Kali turned as Brodie reappeared in the corridor with a box of gloves, a roll of hygiene paper and a paper blanket.

Ailsa took them from him, then asked Brodie

to let Caitlyn know what was happening so she would stop sending people through for a moment.

Kali tugged on a pair of gloves, taking the time to focus.

Mr. Logan's breaths were deeply labored and his face was contorted with pain.

"All right, Mr. Logan, we're going to have to give you a couple of injections—"

"Just get on with it, already," he gasped. "I can't bear it much longer and Bess is in the car."

"Your dog will be just fine, Mr. Logan. We can always get Caitlyn to check on her." Ailsa took charge again. "Just lay still for a moment, Sandy, so we can get some of this painkiller into you. You've not got any allergies, have you?"

"What? No, no. I'm fine."

Ailsa took an antiseptic swab off the tray Brodie had prepared and rubbed it along Mr. Logan's left arm. Deftly she inserted the needle, holding the extension tubing out for Kali to put the syringe on. They watched as the morphine left the tubing and went to work, combatting Mr. Logan's acute pain. Kali carefully injected both the morphine and the midazolam, trying to think of something to chat with him about to monitor the effects of the painkiller.

"And how is Bess these days, Sandy?" asked Ailsa, coming to her rescue.

"She's getting on, like me." Sandy chuckled, a slight wince creasing his forehead as he did so.

"And are you still spoiling her rotten?"

"I don't know what you're talking about," he replied with a soft smile. "No point in going daft over a dog, is there?"

"Course not, Sandy. Even such a loyal one like Bess." Ailsa slipped her fingers to Sandy's wrist before whispering across to Kali, "There's a monitor in the exam room there—the one Brodie's in. Would you mind—?"

"Absolutely. No problem." Kali glanced at her watch as she rose. She could tell by the gentle slurring in Sandy's voice that the painkiller was kicking in...they would just need to wait a few more moments.

Brodie met her at the doorway, portable monitor in freshly gloved hands.

"You're not just standing there earwigging, are you?" Kali quipped.

"Hardly." Brodie's brows tucked closer together, his eyes lighting with a flash of barely contained anger.

Frustration. That was all it was. She'd feel the same.

Kali took the monitor with a smile of thanks.

After Mr. Logan's voice had become incredibly sleepy in response to her questions about how he was feeling, followed by a soft snore, she felt confident to go ahead with the maneuver.

"We're going to have to take your trousers off, Mr. Logan."

Another snore and a soft grunt was her response.

"I think you're all right to proceed, dear." Ailsa smiled.

One look at his face was proof that Sandy Logan didn't care if they dressed him up to look like the Easter bunny as long as his hip was fixed in the process. He wore a goofy grin and was definitely seeing the brighter side of life as the painkillers did their work.

Kali straddled Mr. Logan and raised his hips as Ailsa swiftly tugged off his trousers, offering soothing words of consolation as she did so. Mr. Logan's smile remained intact, his eyes firmly shut.

"Posterior or anterior?" Ailsa asked Kali.

Just one look at the inward pointing knee and foot indicated posterior. For good measure Kali examined the hip, trying to keep her touch as light as possible. The ball joint was very obviously protruding to the rear.

"Posterior." Her years of training took over. "The lower limb will need to be flexed, adducted and internally rotated."

"That's right," Ailsa said, as if her memory had needed jogging as well. If she hadn't been such a great nurse, Kali would've recommended she take up a career in acting.

Kali bent Sandy's knee, tucked her arm in the crook and, with a nod of her head, indicated that

Ailsa should begin applying pressure to the hip as she pressed her heels into the floor and, with a fluid tug and a moan from the semiconscious Mr. Logan, the hip shifted back into place.

Her eyes met Ailsa's and they both laughed with delight.

"I did it!"

"Well done, Dr. O'Shea."

"Nice work."

Kali started at the sound of Brodie's voice. He'd been watching?

"Well…" She shrugged off the compliment. Being in the spotlight had always made her feel uncomfortable.

"Shall we get him onto a backboard and let him have a rest in one of the overnight rooms?" Ailsa asked—the question aimed more at Brodie than Kali.

"Good idea. I'll go get the gear."

"You've got overnight rooms?"

Not a nine-to-five surgery, then. Good. The more all-consuming things were here, the less time she'd have to think about the past. The family she'd left behind. The arranged marriage she'd narrowly avoided.

"A couple." Ailsa nodded. "They're always a good idea, with the weather up here changing at the drop of a hat and…" she nodded at their patient "…for situations like this."

"Thank you."

"For what?" Ailsa looked up at her in surprise.

"You know—for all the help with this. It's all a bit…" As she sought the right word Brodie came back into the corridor with a backboard.

Ailsa gave Kali's arm a squeeze before clearing away the tray of medical supplies, detaching the monitor pads and making room for Brodie to slip the backboard under Mr. Logan at Kali's count.

"Right…" Brodie looked down at the soft smile on Mr. Logan's face. "Glad to see another happy patient. Shall we get him moved before he wakes up and sees I've had anything to do with this?"

"Thank you." Kali looked straight into his eyes. She needed him to know she meant it. "For everything."

"Not a problem. Lift on three?"

He counted at her nod and as they walked Mr. Logan down the corridor she heard Brodie softly laugh to himself.

"What's so funny?"

"I forgot to make your tea."

Three o'clock in the afternoon and still not one patient. Plenty for Kali—but not one had come to see him.

Brodie was about as close to tearing his hair out as he'd ever been. He'd finally managed to remember to make cups of tea, only to find Caitlyn had just done a round for everyone. Terrific. He couldn't even get that right!

Brodie was beginning to get a good under-standing of how innocent people on the run must feel.

Criminal.

Here he was, healthy as a professional ath-lete—he knew that because the doctor monitoring him had expressed envy at his level of fitness—and all for what? To lurk around his own surgery in the desperate hope of picking up a few medi-cal crumbs?

At least Kali was getting a good feel for how the surgery worked. She had a smile on her face every time he saw her. Which would be good if he wasn't so desperate for something to do! There was only so much surfing the internet a man could do. He hardly thought this was what his father had meant when he'd made his final request: *Just one year, son. Just give it one year.*

If—and this was a big if—people were just giving him grieving time, didn't they know he'd be far better off grieving by making good on his promise to his father to run the surgery for a year?

Or maybe… No. *Would* he? Would his father have told folk to do this? Give him wide berth?

No. He shook his head resolutely. His father had always championed him. There were few things he was certain of, but his father's undi-vided loyalty was one of them.

A message pinged through on his office computer. He looked at the screen hopefully, despite his best efforts to remain neutral.

Mr. Donaldson—urgent.

A patient?

It was almost silly how happy he felt. A *patient*! He was out of his chair and on his way to Reception before Mr. Donaldson—a long-time patient of both himself and his father—had a chance to change his mind.

When he opened the door his heart sank.

"Dad, are you absolutely sure?" Mr. Donaldson's daughter, Anne, had her back to Brodie and hadn't seen him come in.

"Of course I'm sure. He's my doctor," Mr. Donaldson insisted.

"But…" Anne looked across at Caitlyn—presumably to get some backup—only to find the receptionist was busy on the phone.

Shame, thought Brodie. He would've been curious to see how she reacted to this. He checked himself. The fact Caitlyn had taken the job showed her support. Never mind that she was family and could do with the money. She didn't let fear override her common sense. Or, he conceded, her nan's say-so.

"Now, Mr. Donaldson. What can I do for you today?"

Anne all but recoiled at the sound of his voice, her arm moving swiftly up to cover her mouth.

"You're all right, Anne." Brodie forced himself to stay calm. "I've been cleared. I'm not contagious."

"Oh, I know, Brodie—Dr. McClellan. It's just—" She stopped speaking, her eyes widening in horror—or embarrassment. She widened the gap between the fingers covering her mouth. "It's just that poor nurse who went where you did in Africa is back in hospital…"

Ah…he'd seen the headlines on the internet. Must've hit the broadsheets as well. That explained the hands and arms covering people's mouths. Fresh media scares about recurrences and isolation units and that poor, poor woman. Her courage and generosity was going heavily unrewarded.

"I saw that." Brodie shook his head. "And I was very sorry to hear it. But I can absolutely assure you that is not the case with me."

"Brodie, I would get up to greet you, but…" the elderly gentlemen interjected, pointing at his foot.

Brodie's eyes widened at the sight. A blood-soaked rag was wrapped around the middle of his foot.

"Is that just a wool sock you're wearing there, Mr. Donaldson?"

"Sure is. My foot would've had a boot on as well, but my daughter, here, said you were likely to cut it off and I wasn't going to let that happen. I only just bought them five years ago. Still got miles to go in them yet."

"Dad!" Anne jumped in, forgetting to shield her mouth. "The boot's got a gaping great hole in it now your turf spade's gone through it. It couldn't have done your foot one bit of good to be yanked out of your boot after you pulled the spade out of it."

"You put a turf spade through your boot and into your foot?"

Brodie couldn't help but be impressed. Wielding a spade with that sort of strength would have taken tremendous power. Then again, at eighty-five years of age Mr. Donaldson showed few signs of succumbing to the frailty of the elderly. *Vital* was just about the best description Brodie could conjure.

"Aye, that I did, son—no need to broadcast it round the village."

"I'd take it as a compliment, Mr. Donaldson. Let's get you into my exam room, shall we?" He moved to help him up just as Kali entered the waiting room with a patient's chart.

"Are you coming, Anne?" Mr. Donaldson turned to see if his daughter was behind them.

Brodie saw Kali catch the look of horror on Anne's face at the suggestion.

"Can I help?" Kali stepped forward without waiting for an answer, offering another arm for

Mr. Donaldson to lean on. Brodie gave her a grateful smile.

This was tough. He'd had a few other doctors warning him something like this might happen, but he'd just blown it off. Dunregan was his *home*! He hadn't expected a victory parade— but having people frightened of being treated by him…? It seared deeper than he'd ever have anticipated.

"Thank you, dear." Mr. Donaldson's fingers wrapped round Kali's forearm. "I'm sure you're busy, but you wouldn't mind, would you?" He raised his voice as they were leaving the waiting room. "Explaining to my daughter that John McClellan's son is *not* going to give me or anyone else who sets foot on Dunregan the plague."

Brodie's eyebrows shot up. An unlikely champion! He had known Mr. Donaldson his whole life, but they certainly weren't close. Then again…he didn't know how many hours of chess had passed between Mr. Donaldson and his father down at the Eagle and Ram. Thousands. Most likely more.

"I'd be delighted to," Kali replied. "Public health is one of my areas of interest."

"As well it should be." Mr. Donaldson nodded approvingly. "Now, you do know, dear," Mr. Donaldson continued, putting his paper-skinned hand atop hers as they inched their way along the corridor, "that Brodie, here, is one of the island's most eligible bachelors?"

"Well, that *is* news!" Kali's eyebrows shot up and...was that a fake smile or real one?

"Yes, it's absolutely true. Isn't that so, Brodie? Most of the suitable girls have already been married off, and we know he will need someone who's a bit of a brainbox to keep him interested. So..."

He didn't wait for an answer. Brodie was too gobsmacked to intervene. Since when had Mr. Donaldson been made the Matchmaker of Dunregan?

"You cannae go far wrong if you marry a Scot, Dr. O'Shea. They're loyal, truehearted... and, of course, if you're into strapping laddies our Brodie here looks very nice when he's all kitted out in his kilt."

"I—I will take you at your word on that," Kali replied, her expression making it very clear she wasn't interested.

"Mr. Donaldson—" Brodie was goldfishing, trying to search for the best way to cut this conversation short. His romantic escapades—and that was about as far as he'd ever taken any of his relationships—were things he'd always kept very close to his chest. Talking about it so openly made him feel about twelve!

"Brodie, why don't you invite Dr. O'Shea, here, along to one of our Polar Bear outings?

They're great fun and a wonderful way to really get to know one another. I've seen more than a few Polar Bear weddings!" He hooted at the memory, then chided Brodie, "And it's been some time since we've seen you down at the beach."

Something in the neighborhood of ten years!

"We should just be taking a left here, Mr. Donaldson." Brodie tried to steer his patient and the conversation firmly off the topic of marriage. He had more than enough on his plate without worrying about getting a fiancée as well.

Not that Kali would be a bad choice, but—

His eyes caught hers. Her expression gave little away. If not the slightest hint of *Uh-uh...you can keep your Scottish yenta.*

"So, Dr. O'Shea," Mr. Donaldson continued, clearly enjoying himself, "you'll do me the favor, please, of going back out there and informing my daughter and the rest of that mob that I've not set to with a fever or anything, won't you?"

"I'll do my best, Mr.—"

"Donaldson. And my daughter is Anne. Now, which way am I going, son?"

"To the left, Mr. Donaldson," Brodie repeated with a shake of his head and a smile. Life on a small island, eh?

Kali looked perfectly bemused, and who could blame her? Not on the island twenty-four hours and already she was being set up by the locals. He sniggered, thinking of how animals always tried to widen the gene pool when their numbers dwindled. Maybe Mr. Donaldson was trying to increase the population of Dunregan. *Ha!*

Kali shot him a look. Whoops. Had that been an outside laugh?

"Later..." he stage-whispered. "I will explain everything later."

If she was going to carry the lance for him regarding the Ebola virus he owed her. As for the whole eligible bachelor thing... Well... At least Mr. Donaldson didn't think he was going to catch the plague.

"Where do you want me?"

"Just over here, Mr. Donaldson. Kali, would you mind helping me get our most loyal and true-hearted patient up onto the examination table?"

"Oh, son. Don't go about trying to set *me* up with this young lassie because I've embarrassed you. That's what old people *do*. It's our specialty. My courting days are over. Mrs. Donaldson was more than enough woman for me," Mr. Donaldson scolded as he eased himself up onto the table. "Let's look at this foot, if you don't mind. What a silly old codger! I was away with the faeries when I was cutting the peat and there was a two-hour wait to see Dr. O'Shea. All this silliness going on over you and the Ebola nonsense..." He shook his head at the madness of it all. "As if someone could contract Ebola on an island this cold!"

He looked at the pair of them for agreement that his hypothesis was a good one.

"Well, it doesn't really work like that..." Brodie began reluctantly.

"Ach, away! I know perfectly well how it works, Brodie McClellan. I was trying to make a joke. Your face is more somber than most folk look at a funeral! Yours, too, dear."

He gave a little cackle and patted Kali's hand as she helped him shift his legs up onto the examination table.

"You go on out there, dear, and please explain—very loudly—to my daughter that no one is catching Ebola on this island if Dr. McClellan says so. John McClellan's son would do no such thing."

Brodie looked away, surprised at the hard sting of emotion hitting him.

Even after he'd passed his father was still looking after him.

He cleared his throat and refocused his attention when he felt Kali shift her gaze from Mr. Donaldson's twinkling eyes up to him. There was something almost anxious in her expression. Something he couldn't put his finger on. And just as quickly it was gone, replaced by a warm, generous smile.

"It would be my very distinct pleasure to answer any of your daughter's questions, Mr. Donaldson."

"Thank you very much. All right, then, dear. Leave us men folk to inspect my idiocy. I'd like to get it bandaged up so I can get the rest of the peat in without the whole of Dunregan knowing I rent my foot in half."

Kali left the room, throwing a final smile over her shoulder at the pair of them. A smile that awoke an entirely new set of sensations in Brodie. He'd done little to nothing to deserve the understanding she'd shown him today.

"Aye, she's a right fine lassie. Isn't she, Dr. McClellan?"

"What?" Brodie turned his attention back to Mr. Donaldson.

"You're not suggesting I'm losing my eyesight as well, are you, son?"

"Absolutely not, but—"

"But nothing. When someone like that arrives on the island, you take notice."

They both turned to look at the closed door, as if it would offer some further insight, but no. It was just a door, covered in various and sundry health notices and how-to sheets. No lessons in romance, or changing terrible first impressions.

Brodie closed down that thought process. Kali wasn't here to be wooed. Or won. And he had a patient!

"Right, Mr. Donaldson…when was the last time you had a tetanus booster?"

CHAPTER FOUR

"It's NOTHING FANCY, but the pub does good, honest food." Brodie loaded Kali's bike onto the rack atop his four-by-four in a well-practiced move. She put her arms up in a show of helping, but he'd clearly done this before.

"I'd rather that than a bad meal of fripperies!"

Brodie laughed as he tugged the security straps tight. "I'm not entirely sure if fripperies are a food group, but I can assure you, you won't get any up here." He opened the car door for her with a slight bow. "Madam?"

Kali felt herself flush, instantly thanking the short days for the absence of light. She climbed in and busied herself with the seat belt buckle to try and shake off an overwhelming urge to flirt. Her gut and her brain were busy doing battle. She *never* wanted to flirt with people…and now she was getting all coquettish with Mr. Disagreeable. Ridiculous!

Probably just her empathy on overdrive. The man had had a tough day. It was natural to want to comfort someone who was hurting, right?

An image of Brodie laying her across a swathe of sheepskin rugs in front of a roaring fire all but blinded her. She clenched her eyes tight, only to find Brodie hiding behind her eyelids—peeling his woolen jumper off in one fluid move, his lean torso lit only by the golden flicker of flames.

Was this what *choice* was? The freedom to choose who you loved?

Loved?

Pah! Arranged marriage was how things worked in the world she'd grown up in. Love was…a frippery. Icing on the cake if your father's choice for your intended turned out to be a good match. Unlike hers. She shuddered at the thought.

Love.

The island air must be giving her brain freeze or something.

She yelped when the driver's door was yanked open. Brodie jumped in and banged his door shut with a reverberating clang.

"The catch on the door is a bit funny," Brodie explained with an apologetic grin. "Suffice it to say Ginny's seen better days."

"Ginny?"

"This grotty old beast."

"Ah…" she managed, still trying to scrub the mental image of her dark past and a half-naked Brodie out of her mind's eye.

Perhaps Mr. Donaldson had put one too many subconscious ideas into motion. This sort of thing had never happened to her in Dublin. Then again…she tipped her head against the cool window as Brodie fired up the engine…in Dublin she'd never felt entirely safe. Up here…

"Now, I should warn you…" Brodie began cautiously.

What? That you've got three girlfriends on the go and the idea of another is repellent?

"Yes?" Kali asked in her very best neutral voice.

"I haven't exactly been to the pub since this whole stramash kicked off."

"Stramash?"

"Sorry. It's Scots for a rammie."

"Still not following you." Her smile broadened. She could listen to Brodie talk forever. All those rolling *r*'s and elongated vowels with a pair of *the most* beautifully shaped lips forming each and every— Oops! Tune in!

"A bit of bother. Or in this case a *big* bit of bother."

"We could always go somewhere else."

Brodie threw back his head and laughed. It was a rich, warm sound. Kali liked the little crinkles that appeared alongside his blue eyes.

Another time, another place…

Another lifetime was more like it. Not with the steamer trunks full of baggage she was hauling around.

"Darlin', this time of year there really *isn't* anywhere else. It's the Eagle and Ram or a fish and chips takeaway from Old Jock's. That's yer choices." He tacked on a cheesy grin for added salesmanship.

"I'm happy with whatever you choose."

"Well…" He gave her a duplicitous wink. "Shall we risk the pub and see if the Ebola public-awareness campaign you kicked off with Anne Donaldson has had any effect beyond the reaches of our humble clinic? It's a bit warmer than a picnic table outside Old Jock's."

Kali nodded, grinning at his choice of words. *Our clinic.*

It had a nice ring to it. Chances were slim he'd meant anything by it, but the words warmed her. Not just because her hormones had decided to kick into action and turn her tummy into a butterfly hothouse, but because she'd never had a chance to be a part of anything in that way before. Put down roots.

Dunregan was the first place she'd been that had absolutely no connection to her past. It was why she'd applied for the so-called hardship post. Safe place was more like it. There was no way her father could find her here, up in the outer reaches of Scotland's less populated islands.

"Right." Brodie pulled the four-by-four in front of a low-slung stone building. "Here goes nothing!"

Moments later Brodie was pulling open a thick wooden door to reveal a picture-postcard pub.

The Eagle and Ram was duck-your-head-under-the-beams old. Being short was an advantage here—unfortunately for Brodie. Kali took in stone walls as deep as her arm. A clientele who looked as though they'd known the place since the rafters were green. A landlady robust enough to turf out anyone who wasn't playing by the rules.

She turned her head at the sound of male voices coming in from the back door. Nope. Scratch the chaps-only presumption. There was a varied clientele. A group of young men kitted out in all-weather gear were clustered round the bar, greeting the landlady familiarly, jokes and banter flying between them and the chaps with flat caps already at the bar. And a couple of ruddy-cheeked women elbowing past the rowdy crew to order drinks.

And then…a complete hush as all eyes lit upon Brodie.

"All right, lads?" Brodie stepped into the room with a broad smile. His physical demeanor looked relaxed, although Kali thought she could hear a tightness in his voice.

Her eyes flicked to a nearby table where a newspaper's headline screamed out the poor nurse's recurrence of Ebola.

A few of the men nodded and a couple of muttered "all rights" slid onto the floor and pooled around their ankles, as if weighing everyone down with the lack of truth in them. The atmosphere was tense. Quite the opposite of all right.

"I've brought the new GP along—Dr. O'Shea—to meet you. Thought I'd give her an Eagle and Ram welcome."

Kali was half-hidden behind Brodie, and felt like hiding herself entirely behind his broad back. She hated the limelight. But something told her she needed to step up and be seen—no matter how much it frightened her. This moment wasn't about *her*.

"Right you are, Brodie." The fifty-something woman came out from behind the bar and stood between them and the ten or so men around the bar. "You're looking well."

"Thank you, Moira. I am feeling fit as a fiddle."

"So I hear. It's the *English* Health Authority, is it? Cleared you to come away back up to Dunregan?"

"That's right."

"The Scottish Health Council no good for you, then?" Her face was serious but her tone carried a teasing lilt.

Brodie nodded, clearly appreciative of what was going on. An impromptu public forum. With pints of beer.

"What do the Scots know about getting sick? Healthy as oxen—the lot of you." His eyes scanned the crowd, then returned to Moira. "Excepting the odd run-in with a peat spade. I take it you've spoken with Anne, then?"

Ding! A lightbulb went on in Kali's head. Moira bore an uncanny resemblance to Anne Donaldson.

"Oh, aye. She rang after she brought Dad back from the clinic. We heard all about it. And about Dr. O'Shea answering all of Anne's questions." The landlady's words were loaded with meaning.

Brodie raised his eyebrows. "Well, good. Your father'll heal up in no time. And there'll be no mention of him coming to the clinic." He tapped his finger on the side of his nose with a *got it* gesture. "That peat came in without incident, right?"

Moira nodded and grinned. "Understood. Good to see you looking so chipper…and healthy. Especially with all you've been through after your father passing and everything—right, boys?"

There was a fresh wave of murmurs and nods—and focus was realigned on what really mattered. To Brodie, at the very least.

"Now, what do you say you two go over by the snug and I'll bring you some nibbles? The fire's on."

Kali followed Brodie's gaze. The snug was way across the other end of the pub and could be closed off with a very thick door.

"I suspect you two'll be talking business, and you won't want us butting our noses in while you get to know each other a bit better," Moira clarified.

Kali got a whiff of matchmaking about the suggestion rather than using the snug as an isolation room. What *was* it with these people and pairing her off?

"That'd be grand, Moira. After you, Kali." Brodie stepped to the side and put out his hand for Kali to lead the way.

She felt her cheeks go crimson, with all pairs of eyes trained on her. *Just smile!* She forced her lips to tip upwards and met one or two sets of eyes. She received nods and a couple of hellos as she passed.

How could walking across a room take an eternity? Her eyes shifted to the floor. The thick wooden planks were covered every now and again with old tin signs. A brand of beer here. A vegetable vendor there. It felt like walking over history while making history. She had no doubt this moment would be talked about.

A headline popped into her head:

Ebola Doc Enters Pub for First Time with Blushing Bride...

Locum! *Locum*. She'd meant to say locum. In her head. Where she was busy lecturing herself in turbo speed.

She felt the color in her cheeks deepen as she scuttled to enter the snug ahead of Brodie. Being in the public eye wasn't ideal when very inappropriate thoughts were charging through her head.

"Oh, look," Brodie stage-whispered. "How romantic! We get it all to ourselves!"

It wasn't until she whirled around to face him, a positively goofy smile of expectation lighting up her features, that she realized he was aiming the comment to the crowd of earwiggers over at the bar.

Now officially mortified, she sank into a cushioned bench seat across from the huge inglenook fireplace, feigning total absorption by the flickering flames. Looking into those crystal clear blue eyes of his just might tip her over the edge.

A bit prickly? Definitely. But his edginess had a depth to it. Like an errant knight slaying dragons only he could see.

"What can I get you to drink?"

Kali nearly jumped in her seat. "You're going to go back out there?" Her fingers flew to her lips. She hadn't meant to say that out loud.

"Absolutely." Brodie gave a wide grin, as if energized by the thought of going back into the lion's den. "Moira's laid the groundwork for my reentry into society here at the pub. And I owe a debt of thanks to you for your handiwork at the clinic today, so no point in turning this into an 'us and them' situation, eh?"

She nodded. Absolutely right. The less acrimony, the better.

See? Errant knight. She gave a satisfied sniff of approval.

"Besides…" He dropped a duplicitous wink. "Now that you've seen all there is to see of the bright lights of Dunregan, I'm guessing the sooner you get back to civilization the better. Am I right?"

Hmm…okay. So he could do with a few tweaks.

"I'm sure I could bear to stay for the duration." She had to force a bit of bravura to her tone. The thought of losing her job before she'd barely begun brought home just how many eggs she'd unwittingly put into the Dunregan basket.

All of them.

Brodie tilted his head, taking a none-too-subtle inspection of the impact of his words. "Easy there, tiger. I'm not doubting your staying power." He laughed. "This is nothing to do with your GP skills. You've proved, beyond a doubt, you can hold your own at the clinic. I just can't imagine why anyone would want to stay up here if they didn't have to."

She pasted on a smile.

It's the first time I've felt safe in years.

"Hey…"

Brodie reached across the table, covering her hand with his. The warmth of his hand worked its way through hers, sending out rays of comfort.

"Honestly, Kali. It was just a joke. If you think I can go in there, order a couple of drinks and change the minds of all those knuckleheads in one night, you're in for a surprise. Apart from being emotional Neanderthals, these folk are stubborn. They put mules to shame."

She managed an appreciative snort. "Sounds like the voice of experience."

"Who knows?" He withdrew his hand and shrugged. "They might take so much of a shine to the new GP you'll be stuck here forever."

Kali chewed on her lip, preventing too broad a smile from breaking out. "Would a wine spritzer be all right?"

"A few shots of whiskey would be more understandable after the day you've had," Brodie intoned, his eyebrows doing an accompanying up and down jig.

"What? You mean sorting out the irascible Young Dr. McClellan? Child's play." She arched an eyebrow expectantly.

"Got it in one!" Brodie laughed appreciatively. *What was going on with her? She didn't flirt. Or behave like a sassy minx. And yet...*

Suffice it to say her tummy was alight with little ribbony twirls of approval.

"Hold that thought. I'll just get the drinks. Wish me luck?"

He dropped another one of those slow-motion,

gorgeous winks, sending the ribbony twirls into overdrive.

"Thank you."

Oh, gross. Did you just coo?

Brodie quirked an eyebrow. "Not a problem."

When he had safely disappeared out of the snug, Kali buried her head in her hands with a low groan. What was going *on* with her? She'd have to have a little mind-over-matter discussion with herself later on. All by herself in the dinky stone cottage she'd rented. The one that didn't strictly have any heat. Or much in the way of windows. But there was a nice sofa!

Hey, she reminded herself, it's home. For this month, at least, it's home.

"So…" A wine spritzer slid across the table into her eyeline a few moments later. "Let's hear it, then."

She sat up, pleased to see Brodie looking unscathed by his trip to the bar.

"Hear what?" Kali took a sip of her spritzer.

"Your life story."

She tried her best not to splutter, and if he'd noticed, Brodie gave nothing away.

"Oh, nothing much to tell." She trotted out the practiced line whilst feeling an unfamiliar tug to tell him the truth.

"I doubt that," Brodie retorted amiably.

"Nothing out of the ordinary," she lied. "Childhood, medical school and now a locum position up here."

It was staggering how much had happened in between each of those things. Her father's vow to avenge the family's honor when she'd backed out of the match he'd made for her. The terrifying flight for her life with a fistful of cash. So much...*too* much...for a young woman to carry on her shoulders. If it hadn't been for the government's ability to give her a new identity—

Enough.

Those were her stories to keep safely hidden away.

"Is that a bit of an Irish accent I detect?" Brodie wasn't giving up.

"Yes." She nodded. "I did my medical degree in Dublin." That much was true.

"But you grew up in England?"

She nodded, taking a deep drink of her spritzer.

"No matter what I do, or what corner of the world I find myself in, I can't seem to shake my accent." Brodie shook his head as he spoke.

Why would he want to? Brodie's accent was completely and totally gorgeous. Which she wasn't going to tell him, so best change the subject.

"So...you've traveled a lot?"

"Some." He nodded. "Lots, actually. Unlike everyone else who was born and raised here, I couldn't wait to get off the island."

"Why?"

"Is it so hard to believe?"

"Yes!" Kali nodded her head rigorously. "I think Dunregan's great."

"Aye, well…" His eyes shot off to that faraway place she couldn't access. "You don't have history here."

Fair enough. She had her own history, and no one was going to pry that from her.

"Where have you traveled?" she asked.

"Everywhere I could at first."

"At first?"

"My father always hoped I'd take over the clinic after medical school, but I…" He paused for a moment searching for the right words. "I struggled to *settle* here."

There was a reason behind that. That much was clear. One only he would decide when to reveal.

Kali was about to say something, but clamped her lips tight when Brodie continued without prompting.

"I'd do stints here, to help relieve my father. The job is bigger than one man's best. Especially during tourist season. But over the winter I kept finding myself volunteering abroad. Orphanages, refugee camps needing an extra pair of hands, villages without access to hospitals." He laughed suddenly, his eyes lighting up. "I used up the paltry first aid kit the agency gave us in my first couple of weeks away! Got my dad to send more supplies along whenever I changed country…"

His eyes shifted to the fire, his brow crinkling as something darker replaced the bright acuity of the happy memory.

Kali pulled him back to the present with a question about his work in Africa. Then another. And before she knew it their conversation had lifted into something effortless and taken flight.

Time slipped away with stories shared and anecdotes compared as their mutual passion for medicine carried them away from whatever had encumbered them during the day into the undefinable giddy excitement that came from meeting a—*a soulmate.*

Kali froze at the thought, her gaze slipping to Brodie's hands. His fingers loosely circled his pint, one index finger shifting along the dewy sheen of condensation as he told her about his grandfather and the crew of men he'd corralled into helping him build the stone clinic in exchange for some of his wife's shortbread. It was how folk did things up here, Brodie was saying. Together. Always together.

And she'd spent her entire adult life alone.

Was a soulmate something she even deserved after leaving her mother and sister behind with her father?

"…and then, when he retired up to the mountains, the key was passed on to my father," Brodie concluded with an affectionate smile. "I don't know if I've told anyone the whole story in one go before. You must've bewitched me with your beguiling ways!"

Kali laughed shyly, her eyes flicking up to meet Brodie's. When their gazes caught and meshed she felt her body temperature soar as the magnetic pull of attraction multiplied again and again, until she forced herself to look away and pretend it hadn't happened.

"So, you coming back here to run the clinic is kismet, really, isn't it?"

She saw him blink away something. A memory, perhaps. Or a responsibility he had neither asked for nor wanted.

She tried again. "Or was it more preordained?"

"Something like that." He took another drink of his pint, eyebrows furrowing. "Look, Kali... while I'm on a bit of a very uncharacteristic 'tell all' roll, I think you should know something— something about *me*. Because you'll no doubt hear it at some point while you're here and I'd rather you heard it from me."

Her heart lurched to her throat as her chin skidded off her hand. Had he felt it, too? The click of connection that made her feel as if she could find sanctuary in telling him who she really was?

She sat as still as she could, her fingers woven

together in front of her on the wooden table as he began.

"When I was about ten I went out on a sailboat with my mother. Begged her, actually. She and I hadn't been out since my kid brother had been born." He cleared his throat roughly. "Long story short: the weather turned nasty. Our boat got overturned. I made it back. My mother didn't."

Kali's fingers had clenched so tightly as he spoke her flesh had turned white with tension.

"Oh, Brodie. I am *so* sorry."

He shook his head. "No, I didn't tell you for your pity. I just want you to understand why sticking around this place isn't top of my list."

"Then why are you here? If there are so many bad memories?"

"A promise." He circled his fingers round his pint, weaving them together on the far side and moving them back again. "To my dad. He loved it here so much and wants—*wanted*—the same for me. So he asked me to stay for a whole year. No trips, no inner-city assignments, a year solid on the island. And I think he wanted someone—family—to be here to look after Callum. My brother," he added.

"And after the year is up—was he expecting you to close the clinic or hand it on to someone else?"

Was this where she came in?

"Ha! No." Brodie smiled at her as if she were

an innocent to the world of hard knocks, then his expression softened. "I suppose it was his not very subtle way of hoping I'd fall back in love with the place."

"How's that working out for you?" Kali chanced in a jokey tone.

"Absolutely brilliantly, Dr. O'Shea! Nothing like winning over the people you've kept at arm's length all your life with a nice little Ebola scare." He raised his glass and finished his pint in one long draught.

"You know…" Kali said after they'd sat for a minute in silence. "What's happening here…with you, the islanders…it's really quite exciting."

Brodie couldn't help but laugh. "You've always got a positive spin on things, don't you, Kali? Is this excitement you speak of manifesting itself in the way nary a soul would step foot in the clinic until you arrived, or in the way they've stuck us in this room where no one hardly ever goes except to read the paper in a bit of peace?"

"See—that's where you've got it all wrong."

Her green eyes shone with excitement, as if she had a huge secret she was about to share. If anyone else had told him he'd got it wrong he would've bridled. But coming from Kali…?

It seemed completely bonkers, but he felt closer to her after just a handful of hours than he had near enough anyone outside of his family.

Beguiled or bedeviled?

He didn't know what it was, but he was spilling private thoughts like it was going out of style. And a part of him felt…*relief.* As if with the telling of his story he'd somehow lessened the levels of internal pain it caused.

"I don't mean it in a bad way, Brodie. It's just—you're taking the reaction of the villagers incredibly personally. Which, obviously, it would be hard not to. *But*," she continued quickly, before he could jump in to protest, "it seems to me people are using the Ebola thing as an excuse."

He grunted a go-on-I'm-listening noise.

"Now that I know why you don't want to be here, I get it. That's a lot of weight to carry on your shoulders for something you surely realize wasn't your fault."

She held up her hand again, making it clear he was going to have to hear her out—gutsy beguiler that she was.

"Perhaps—and this is just a *perhaps*—everyone here thinks you've turned your back on *them*. Your job is to help people. Help them at a time when they're feeling weak, or frightened or downright awful. And if you add a bit of fear into the mix…fear that you won't be around when they've entrusted you with their private concerns…"

"It makes for a pretty poisonous pill," he finished, seeing his plight from an entirely new angle. "I see where you're going with this," Brodie admitted with a nod.

He was so intent on ticking days off the calendar to get through the year he was blinded to everything else. But he wanted to fulfill his promise honorably—so until he took full control of the clinic he couldn't mark a single day off the calendar. He scrubbed at his hair and jiggled his empty pint glass back and forth. Maybe that was why everyone was refusing to see him. So he could never turn over the hourglass and begin the countdown.

He gave her an impressed sidelong look. "You sure you didn't specialize in psychology?"

"Positive."

Kali flushed as their eyes met. A sweet splash of red along the porcelain lines of her cheekbones. She was a beautiful woman. And smart.

Frustration and anger had eaten away at his ability to be compassionate. Show the people he'd known his entire life the same care and attention he'd given each and every patient he'd treated abroad. The same care and attention they'd shown him when first he'd lost his mother and then again when his father had passed. Even if they weren't all huggy-kissy about it.

Anonymous plates of scones had been delivered. Stews heated up. Distance kept...

"You're quite the insightful one, Dr. O'Shea."

"Well..." She drew a finger round the base of

her wine glass. "We've all had hurdles to jump. I know how frustrating it can be when it seems like no one is on your side. You against the world, sort of thing. But it's not exactly as if you're powerless to change things, is it?"

Something told Brodie she was talking about something a world away from what *he* was experiencing. An instinct told him not to push. His were the only beans getting spilled tonight.

"I get the feeling you have an idea or two about how I can win the hearts and minds of my fellow islanders." Brodie leaned forward, rubbing his hands together in a show of anticipation.

"I do!" she chirped, enthusiasm gripping her entire body. "GPs are at the forefront of the medical world as far as a community like this is concerned, right? They're authority figures, really."

Brodie nodded. He'd always pictured his father as the authority, but now he supposed that baton had been well and truly handed over.

"And what do you see me doing with all of this authority?"

"Well...it sounds like you've had some amazing experiences overseas. You combine that with your local knowledge and you've got an amazing opportunity for public outreach. To teach people firsthand what's going on in the world beyond the sensationalist headlines." She picked up a discarded copy of the nation's favorite rag and held it in front of him like a red cape to a bull. "Make them wise, not reactionary. From Ebola to...to Zika virus."

"What? Quell their fears about Ebola, only to get everyone up in arms about every mosquito arriving on their hallowed shores being laden with the Zika virus? Now *there's* an idea?"

Kali swatted at the space in between them, taking his words as he'd meant them. In jest. With a healthy splash of affection.

The strangest feeling overtook him as he watched her speak. He was no spooky-spooky sort, but meeting Kali felt meant to be. Their long talk, which had all but emptied the pub, seemed like a homecoming of sorts—as if they'd been cinching the loose strings of a relationship they'd let fade and were now eager to rekindle.

Her own voice came to him in the perfect way to describe the sensation.

Kismet.

And then he realized she was still talking about public awareness.

"You know what I mean. The only reason people are being funny about you is because they don't understand. About Ebola. Why you don't like it here. And, frankly, I'm a little on their side with that one. You're keeping them at arm's length. It makes you scarier."

"Loveable, approachable me?" Brodie put

on his best teddy bear face. "I come across as *scary*?"

"Yes! Exactly!" She grinned, her smile lighting up those green eyes of hers from within.

Funny how a guy could take an insult when it came from a woman with such a genuine smile.

"Luckily I've already learned your bark is worse than your bite," Kali replied regally.

She was obviously enjoying herself. The young medical disciple offering words of wisdom to the block-headed Scottish doctor.

"So...how do you suggest I open my arms to people who don't even want to breathe the same air as me?"

"Get a gas mask," she replied with a straight face.

He stared at her, waiting to see if she'd break. She didn't.

"A gas mask? That's your big idea."

Kali burst into gales of laughter, tears of delight filling the rims of eyes now flecked with golden reflections of the fire.

"Sorry, sorry..." She swallowed away the remains of her giggles, pressing her lips together in an attempt to regroup. "Look. You don't have to do it alone. I'm happy to go to bat for you."

"So soon?" He feigned astonishment, though in truth he was genuinely touched.

"Oh, it's more for me than you," she replied with mock gravitas. "I don't know if you noticed, but there's an awful backlog of patients to see. Time is of the essence, Dr. McClellan."

Brodie grinned. Couldn't help it. Probably his first genuine smile since he'd lost his father. "Anyone told you your enthusiasm is infectious, Miss O'Shea?"

"That's *Dr.* O'Shea to you," she riposted with a shy smile.

He tipped his head to the side and looked at her with fresh eyes.

Strikingly pretty. Petite, but not fragile. Thick mane of black hair framing the soft outlines of her heart-shaped face. And those eyes...

He'd better watch it. This whole two-peas-in-a-pod thing had *wrong time, wrong place* written all over it.

"So, what do you say?" He rubbed his hands together briskly. "We take on the islanders one by one, or gather them all up in a stadium and do it warlord-style?"

"I was thinking more softly, softly—kitten-style."

"You think I'm up to being a *kitten*?" Brodie snorted as Kali feigned imagining him as a kitten.

"Maybe more of an alley cat. With an eye patch and a broken tail."

"Ah—so we'll have a cat fight at the end?"

"*Purrr*haps," she purred, completely capturing his full attention.

Her lips were parted, chin tilted up toward his,

eyelids lowered, half cloaking that mystical green-eyed gaze of hers as a thick lock of hair fell along her cheek. He was itching to shift it away, feel the peachy softness of her skin.

Brodie readjusted as his body responded.

Kali had just shape-shifted from beautiful to downright sexy.

And an instant later...the shutters closed.

Kali's gaze had gone from inviting to *stay away* in an actual blink of the eye.

He chalked up another reminder about barriers as she tugged on her coat, pulling the zip right up to her chin.

She wasn't here to stay. Nor was he.

Kali threw her coat on top of the duvet, shivered, then grabbed her suitcase and shook the whole pile of clothes along the bed in a line stretching the length of her body.

Her fire-making skills, as it turned out, were not great. Thank goodness she'd convinced Brodie to let her ride her bicycle home in lieu of a lift, otherwise she'd have no body heat at all! Not that he hadn't put up a fight.

He'd insisted. She'd insisted more firmly. Said it was all part of the rugged island adventure she'd been banking on when she took up the post. She tugged on a pair of tights and zipped a fleece over her layers of T-shirts and jumpers, acutely aware that an online shopping spree was growing increasingly essential.

Her eyes flicked over to the bedroom door. Firmly shut. Front door? Dead-bolted. Checked twice. She'd never let anyone walk, drive or cycle home with her in the past five years. The fewer people who knew where she lived the better. And yet...

How many times had she been tempted to blurt out her life story tonight?

Too many.

How many times had she let herself wonder... *what if*?

Each time she'd caught herself staring at Brodie's lips was how many.

Too many.

This was a working relationship. Not an island romance.

Apart from which, Brodie wanted nothing to do with Dunregan and she...she wanted *everything* to do with it. Just one day here was as appealing as one day with her "intended" had been repellent.

She huffed out a sigh of exasperation, eyes widening as she did.

Was that her *breath*?

She pulled up the covers, trying to keep the pile of clothes balanced on top of her, and snuggled into the fetal position. Shivering created body warmth.

She giggled. Now she was just being silly. But it felt good. She hadn't been plain old silly in… *years*. Perhaps it was the cold, or the delicious lamb stew she'd virtually inhaled at the Eagle and Ram. She felt warm from the inside. A cozy glow keeping the usual fears at bay.

She was safe here in Dunregan. And, for tonight at least, she couldn't wipe the smile off her lips if she tried.

CHAPTER FIVE

Too late, Brodie saw the beginning of the end. It was a miracle the wood had stayed atop his four-by-four this far.

"Nooooooooo!"

The planks of wood were crashing and slithering all over the place. Smack-dab in front of the clinic.

He glanced at his watch.

Kali would be there soon. No doubt expressing her despair at yet another way he'd made her time at the clinic less than straightforward.

Three days in and she seemed a more regular part of the place than he ever had. Correction. Than he had ever *felt*.

Big difference.

He nudged a bit of wood with his foot and shook his head.

Woodworking was a class he really should have taken when he'd had the chance. He'd scoffed at his brother's choice at the time. Now he was beginning to see the advantages of having learned some practical skills. Or having stuck around so he could've built the blasted thing with his father, a man as at home with a hammer as a stethoscope.

He heard a throat clearing on the far side of his car.

Kali.

Kali trying desperately not to laugh.

She'd been keeping him at a courteous arm's length after their strangely intimate night at the pub, so it was nice to see that smile of hers.

"New project?" she asked, barely able to contain her mirth.

"Aye. I'm sure you will have noticed just sitting round the clinic waiting for patients to magically appear hasn't worked quite the treat I'd hoped."

She made a noncommittal noise, turning her head this way and that, obviously trying to divine what the pile of wood in front of her—*his*—clinic was meant to be.

"It's a boat."

"Ohhhh…" She nodded. "I can see that now."

"Ha-ha. Very funny."

"No, I mean it." She sidled up beside him, crossed her arms and gave the hodgepodge pile of wood a considered look before pointing to one of the shorter cuts. "That's the pram, right?"

"The prow," he corrected, the language of boats coming back to him as if it were genetically embedded.

"And you're building this here because…?" Kali tactfully changed the subject.

"I was rehashing our talk the other night— about public awareness and all that—and I thought, how can I get through to everyone island-style?"

"And this is what you came up with?" Kali gave him a dubious look.

"I told you—it's a boat." He frowned at the pile of wood. "Or it will be once word gets out I'm trying to make one. The folk here can't resist giving advice when it comes to building a boat."

"And that means you're staying?"

A jag of discord shot through him at the wary note of hope in her voice. He'd heard it often enough in his father's voice each time he'd returned. The thought of disappointing Kali bothered him, but he wasn't there yet. In that place where settling down—setting down *here*—felt right. Might not ever be. That was why he'd decided to get out of the clinic, where they had been warily circling each other after that night of so much connection. No bets taken as to why he was building the boat right next door to the clinic, though.

It was Kali. One hundred percent Kali.

He scrubbed his jaw and tried to look like a model citizen.

"I was thinking more along the lines of the public health campaign first."

She gave him a sidelong glance. One he couldn't read. One that made him wonder if she could see straight through his bluster.

"This is your master plan to convince people you don't have Ebola?"

"Who could resist such a rugged, healthy-looking soul?" Brodie looked off into the middle distance supermodel-style. Sure, he was showing off, but the reward was worth it.

A shy grin.

Each of Kali's smiles was like a little jewel—well worth earning.

He struck a bodybuilder pose to see if he could win another.

Bull's-eye.

A fizz of warmth exploded in Kali's belly. Then another. *Would he just stop doing that?*

"Well? What do you think? Irresistible or repugnant?"

Brodie's blue eyes hit hers and another detonation of attraction hit Kali in the knees. What *was* she? Twelve? *Regroup, girl. This man has danger written all over him.*

"Well…you're not exactly repugnant…"

Brodie threw back his head and laughed. "Touché."

He dropped her a wink. Another knee wobbler.

"Serves me right for floating my own boat." Brodie's eyes scanned the higgledy-piggledy pile of wood. "Or not, as the case might be."

Kali gave him a quick wave and hightailed

it around the back of the building and into the clinic.

Despite her best efforts to keep her nose to the proverbial grindstone...to see patients and race her bicycle back home to her icy cold house...she knew she was falling for Brodie. Fast.

It scared her. But as unsettling as it felt it also felt good. A little *too* good.

He wasn't hanging around. It was easy enough to see the boat was a project with a timeline and once that was done... *Poof.*

Goodbye, Romeo.

Or, more accurately, goodbye, Kali. Brodie would win the hearts of Dunregan back in no time and then there'd be no need for her here. Before she knew it, it would be time for her to begin again.

"Kali?" Ailsa called to her from the tea room as the back door shut with its satisfying click and clunk. "I've just put the kettle on. Milk and no sugar, isn't it?"

"Got it in one!" She grinned despite the storm of unwelcome thoughts.

"Are we going to be blessed with my nephew's presence today?" Ailsa popped her head round the corner and gave Kali an exasperated smile.

"He's out front," Kali answered. "Building a boat."

Ailsa's eyebrows shot up. "Aye?"

Kali nodded, keeping her own expression neutral.

"Well..."

It was a loaded word. Suspicious. Loving. Expectant. Curious.

Kali couldn't help but smile. She might not have much time here, but at the very least she was becoming much more fluent in Scots!

"Kali! First patient's come early!" Caitlyn called from the front office. "Will you be all right to take a look?"

"It would be my pleasure," she replied, accepting the hot cup of tea Ailsa had just handed her. "Let's get this show on the road."

"Someone's up with the lark."

A woman in her early thirties spun round at the sound of the bell ringing above the door, her face lighting up with a smile when she saw it was Kali.

"The usual?"

Kali grinned. This was the third morning running she'd relished the warmth and sugary sweet air of the Dunregan Bakehouse. This first "thawing station" on her bicycle ride into work. It had nothing to do with the fact they also made the fluffiest scones she'd ever tasted. And with lashings of the fruitiest, raspberriest jam in the world. She'd bought treats for everyone at the clinic each day since she'd discovered the place.

"I'm Helen, by the way."

"Nice to meet you. I'm Kali—"

"O'Shea," finished Helen with a laugh. "If you haven't found out already, word travels fast in Dunregan. By my count, you've been here about a week now."

"Only three more to go!"

The words were double-edged. She didn't want to leave. Little bits of her heart were already plastered about the small harbor town. Once she got a chance to explore some more she was sure the rest of it would follow suit.

"I guess you'll know my being here is actually a bit pointless. With Brodie having the all clear." It was hardly subtle, but they'd passed that point.

"I thought he'd given up doctoring to build that boat of his?"

Kali pulled a face. To say Brodie was making a success of turning the pile of planks into a boat would be...very kind. He'd eventually brought all the wood over and laid it out in a completely indecipherable series of piles in the open shed next to the clinic. Some nails had gone in. Some nails had been pulled out. The piles remained.

"I'm no expert on boat building myself, but I get the feeling medicine is more of his forte," she said as tactfully as she could. "But it keeps him busy while he waits for his patients to feel more comfortable about coming back to see him."

Helen laughed conspiratorially, but Kali saw a generous dose of compassion in her brown eyes. "I don't think I ever saw him near the woodworking classes at school. Complete and total brainbox." Distractedly she added a couple more scones to the box she was filling. "You know, I have an idea of someone who could lend a hand. In the meantime…" She flicked the lid shut, putting a Dunregan Bakehouse sticker in place to seal it as she did so. "I've got something special for you to try."

She put up her finger to indicate that she'd be back in a second and disappeared into the back.

"Me?" Kali whispered to the empty room, a giddy twirl of anticipation giving an extra lift to her smile. She knew it was silly, but the gesture made her feel—*better* than welcome. As if she were part of something. A community.

"Right. Give this a taste." A piece of toast appeared in her eyeline. Thick cut, oozing with butter and a generous smear of soft cheese. "You're all right with goat's cheese?"

"Absolutely. I love it." Kali took the bread and was three bites in before she remembered Helen was expectantly waiting for a response. "This is the most delicious thing *ever*," she said through another mouthful. "Ever!"

"Really?" Helen's eyes glowed with happiness. "It's a new bread I've been working on. Hazelnuts and a mix of grains for all the island's health nuts. I'm still debating about raisins. But it's locally produced cheese so I thought I might put it on the board as a lunch offering. What with you being an outsider, I thought you'd give an honest response."

"It's completely yummy."

And thanks for the reminder that I don't belong here. Surprising how much it stung.

"Thanks, Dr. O'Shea."

"Kali," she corrected firmly. They were around the same age. And on the off-chance that she were to stay…

Don't go there. As long as your father is alive, you'll always live a life on the run.

"Thanks, Kali. It means a lot. And don't worry about Brodie's boat. We'll get him sorted out—island-style."

Mysterious. But positive! Kali left the bakery with a wave, feeling a bit unsettled. Could a place do that to someone? Or, she thought, as an image of Brodie flickered through her overactive brain, was it a person that was unsettling her?

"Look who made it all the way up the hill today!" Brodie applauded as Kali dismounted from her bicycle with a flourish. "A mere week on the island and you're a changed woman!"

Kali flushed with pleasure, glad her cheeks were already glowing with exertion.

"It has helped that the wind isn't quite so—"

"Hostile?" offered Brodie.

"Exactly."

Kali smiled at his choice of word, but now she officially needed to get indoors as soon as possible. No heat again in her house meant riding her bicycle and the pit stop at the bakery were the only ways she got warm in the morning. It was absolutely freezing! Which did beg the question...

"How many layers are you wearing?"

"You like?"

Brodie did a little catwalk strut for her. Man, he had a nice bum. A nice *everything*. Even if it *was* covered in a million layers of down and fleece.

"You'll do."

Understatement of the universe!

"So how is Operation Public Awareness going?"

"Well, in terms of gathering in the crowds, you can see how well *that's* going." He swept his arm along the length of the empty street.

"Mmm...could be the weather?"

"Or could be they just prefer you," Brodie replied, his tone lighter than a week ago, when even mentioning the cotton bud delivery had been enough to set him off. Keeping her distance had been easier when he was all grumbly.

This Brodie... All rugged and tool wielding... *Yummy.*

* * *

"What's in the magic basket today?"

Brodie leaned toward the wicker basket he had helped Kali attach to the front of her bike with a whole pack of zip ties. Suffice it to say his stitches were better than his DIY skills.

"Wouldn't you like to know?" She protectively covered the box with her hand, eyes sparkling with excitement.

For a split second Brodie envied her the purity of emotion. Every joy he experienced seemed to come with conditions. Obligation after obligation, intent on dragging him down.

Although lately...

"Don't open it yet." He nodded at the box. "I bet I can sniff it out. I've got a nose that knows..." He tapped the side of it with a sage nod.

Kali laughed, dimpling with the simple pleasure of silly banter.

"It's definitely not bridies hiding in there."

She shook her head, lips pushed forward in a lovely little *guess again* moue.

"Too early for hot cross buns..."

"Correct again." She nodded. "That you're wrong, that is."

"Scones." He took a step back. "That's my final answer."

"Is it, now?"

The *guess again* moue did a little back and forth wiggle.

Suggestive. Very, very suggestive.

She unpeeled the sticker to reveal a pile of fluffy scones. Then snapped the lid shut again before he could get his hand in there to steal one.

"Uh-uh." She wagged a finger at him. "These are for later. For *everyone*."

"You know, you've got to stop spoiling us like this."

"Why?" She looked at him like he was nuts.

"We just might get used to it."

"We?" she countered, with a flirty shift of the hips.

"Me," he admitted, not wanting to put words to the feeling of emptiness he knew was inevitable once she left.

"Go on, now." He shooed her off. "Run off to your lovely warm clinic whilst I freeze to death out here with my pile of wood."

"Take your time," Kali teased. "Gives me more time to steal all of your patients!"

Her grin disappeared instantly at the sight of Brodie's defenses flying into place, blue eyes snapping with anger.

"I'm perfectly happy to come in and see patients. It is, after all, *my* name on the clinic."

The words flew at her like sharp arrows and just as rapidly her own walls of protection slammed down.

Too soon.

She'd let herself believe in the fairy tale too soon.

"I'm perfectly aware it's a temporary posting, all right? I just—" She looked away for a minute, trying to ward off the sting of tears.

She'd been too keen. Too enthusiastic about settling in. Brodie's sharp reaction served her right. She'd fallen hook, line and sinker for the friendly island welcome. The frisson she'd thought existed with Brodie. Her heart had opened up to give too much faith too soon. Trusting people was always a mistake—how could she not know that by now? After everything she'd been through?

Fathers were meant to look after their daughters. Care for them. Protect them. It had never occurred to her that he would choose a man with a history of violence to be her husband. Perhaps her father had fallen for the smooth public demeanor her "intended" had down to a fine art. The one that hid the fact he saw nothing wrong with hitting her to get what he wanted. Her hand flew to her cheek as if the slap had happened yesterday.

She stamped her feet with frustration and forced herself to look Brodie in the eye. It was what people who were in control of their lives did. Met things head-on.

They stood there like two cowboys, each

weighing up whether or not it was safe to holster their weapons.

From the looks of Brodie's expression—a virtual mirror of her own—Kali was fairly certain they were both wishing they could swallow back their words.

Had she been this touchy when she went to the Forced Marriage Protection Unit and pleaded for a new identity? She'd been so consumed with fear and a near-primal need to survive she didn't really have a clue *what* sort of impression she'd given. If Brodie was feeling half the trauma she'd experienced, it was little wonder his temperament was whizzing all over the place.

"I didn't mean to stake some sort of claim on your clinic."

"And I didn't mean to sound like such an ass."

She watched as Brodie raked his long fingers through his thatch of wayward blond hair.

He met her questioning gaze head-on. "Start again…*again*?"

There it was. That melt-her-heart-into-a-puddle smile.

"Sounds good," she managed, without too much of a waver in her voice.

"Shall I make you a cup of tea?"

Kali couldn't help it. She burst out laughing. "The solution to everything? No, thanks, you're all right. I don't want to stand in the way of a man who's got a boat to build!"

Brodie shook off her refusal and commandeered her bicycle, hooking his free arm through hers as he did so, turning them both toward the clinic door. A small step in the right direction to start afresh.

"Now, then, Dr. O'Shea, if I can't make you a fresh cup of tea, I'm not going to be much good at building a boat, am I?"

"I suppose not." Kali giggled. "But how long is this going to take? It did take you about five hours to make me one on my first day."

"Well, lassie…" He increased his brogue, rolling his *r*'s to great effect, mimicking his auntie Ailsa. "Can you afford me a second chance to make you a nice cuppa tea within the hour, accompanied by a wee bit of Mrs. Glenn's delicious shortbread?"

"That would be lovely." Kali smiled up at him, eyes bright, cheeks flushed with the cold and the cycle ride.

Brodie found himself fighting an urge to bend down and kiss her. But getting attached to Kali when he had no idea what his own future held… *Bad idea.*

He unhooked his arm from hers, focusing on getting her bicycle into the stand at the back door. Wooing the locum was probably *not* what his father had had in mind when he'd hoped his son would fall in love with the island.

Besides, Kali wasn't here for an island fling—she was here to do a job. *His* job! And it rankled. Perhaps he wouldn't go inside with her after all.

"Right, then, here you are, Dr. O'Shea. Enjoy your day in the clinic. I've got a boat to build!" He gave her a silly salute he didn't quite feel just as Ailsa poked her head through the door.

"Oh, there you both are. I've been wondering if it was just me who was going to run this place today. Kali, you look like you've just been pried out of an iceberg!"

Brodie took a closer look. "Are you shivering?"

"No. Not really." Kali's lips widened into a wince, only succeeding in making her shivering more obvious.

"Oh, for heaven's sake!" cried Ailsa. "Come in out of the cold, would you? I've just put the kettle on. I'll make us all a nice cuppa tea. And perhaps some of Mrs. Glenn's delicious shortbread."

Kali and Brodie shared a glance, bursting into simultaneous laughter.

Ailsa waved them off as if they'd each lost their wits. "Ach, away with the pair of you. Now, hurry up so I don't heat up the outdoors more than the clinic."

Kali gathered together the day's files, tapped them on the top and sides so they all aligned, then picked them up to give them a final satisfying *thunk* on the desk.

There.

She'd done it.

Another full day of seeing patients—and, she thought with a grin, it had all gone rather swimmingly.

Brodie had been in and out of the tea room, reading various instruction manuals for an ever-growing array of tools. She'd chanced a glance out into the large shed when he'd come in for a cuppa and had smiled at the untouched pile of wood. But she wouldn't have a clue how to build a boat, so she would be the last one to cast aspersions.

Her phone rang through from the reception line.

"Hello, Caitlyn, are you all ready to close up shop for the day?"

"I am, but I was wondering if you wouldn't mind seeing one last patient. Mr. Fairways has popped in. Says his hearing aid is acting up."

"Wouldn't he be—" Kali was going to ask if he'd be better off seeing a hearing specialist, but remembered there was no hospital. "Absolutely." It wasn't as if she had anything else to do. "I'll come out and get him."

She pushed through the door into the waiting room, where a wiry gentleman—an indeterminate fiftysomething, wearing a wax jacket and moleskin trousers—was leaning on the counter, speaking with Caitlyn. He looked familiar to her, but that was hardly likely seeing as she'd only been on the island for a week.

"Mr. Fairways?"

He continued to regale Caitlyn with a blow-by-blow account of the weather. Was that feedback she was hearing? She walked toward him. Yes. There was definitely feedback coming from one of his hearing aids.

"Mr. Fairways?" She touched his shoulder.

"Ah, hello there." He turned to reveal a pair of deep brown eyes and the most wonderful mustache Kali had ever seen outside of a nineteenth-century photo. Or…had she seen him before? There was something familiar about him she couldn't put a finger on.

"So you're the mad spirit who's come up to join us on our fair isle?"

Kali smiled. "Something like that. I understand you're having a problem with your hearing aid?"

A screech of feedback filled the small waiting room.

"What was that, dear?"

Caitlyn stifled a giggle. Kali shot her a horrified look. She couldn't *laugh* at the patients!

"I said, I understand you're here about your hearing aid?"

"I can't quite understand your accent, dear. I'm here about my hearing aid." He glanced at the window facing the street. "I see Young Dr. McClellan is taking a hand to building that boat."

"That's what he says." Kali smiled, then hid her flinch at another piercing hit of feedback.

"What volume do you have your hearing aid on, Mr. Fairways?"

"Eh?"

"The volume?" Kali turned an invisible volume control near her ear.

"Oh, it's up as high as it'll go! It was getting harder to hear so I ramped it right on up."

"That might be your problem."

"Eh?"

Caitlyn out-and-out laughed. Kali hushed her, but not in time for Mr. Fairways not to take notice.

"Oh, you'll want to watch it, lassie." He teasingly waggled a finger in front of the receptionist's eyes. "You might be bonny now, but soon enough you'll be all old and wrinkly like me—eyes not working so well, ears packed up and wondering what on earth people are talking about."

"Ach, away." Caitlyn waved off his comment with a youthful grin. "You're hardly an old codger, Mr. Fairways. My great-gran's about twice your age. You're obviously doing something funny to those hearing aids of yours, though, with the amount of bother they're giving you."

"Since the day I was born, lassie. Since the day I was born."

"So you've *always* had hearing aids?" Kali asked.

"Aye, well…"

Kali smiled. She was getting used to the Scots' all-purpose response. Never giving more information than absolutely necessary. She was hardly one to quibble with the tactic.

"Why don't you come down to my office and we'll take a look?"

A few minutes later Kali had eased down the volume on her patient's hearing aids, syringed his ears and clipped away the long hairs that had accrued outside his ear canal. Once he had the hearing aids safely back in place Kali spoke at a normal volume.

"There doesn't seem to be anything wrong with the hearing aids so far as I can tell, Mr. Fairways, but it's a good idea to keep your ears as clear of hair and wax as you can."

"I know, dearie, but with no one to keep myself dapper for I sometimes forget."

"Well, you're always welcome to come along and see me." As the words came out of her mouth she realized they weren't true. This was temporary. Just like so much in her life had been. Temporarily safe. Temporarily happy. Temporarily a normal woman doing her dream job with a hot Viking building…something or other just outside.

"Aye, well…" Mr. Fairways's brow crinkled with concern.

"Let's make you an appointment with the audiologists next time they're on the island. Unless you usually go to the mainland for this sort of thing?"

"Oh, no. I stay here. I'm the honorary mayor of Dunregan, and it wouldn't do for me to be leaving willy-nilly. I'm happy here. On the island," he qualified, as if that weren't obvious.

"Right, then, so I'll check with Dr. McClellan about the audiologists and we'll get in touch."

"Fine." Mr. Fairways gave a satisfied nod, but made no move to leave.

"Is there anything else you want to talk about?"

"No, no…not really—it's just that…"

"Mmm…?" Kali nodded that he should feel free to speak.

"I just noticed Brodie doesnae have a proper base set up for his A-frames. He won't be getting the right sort of balance on the skiff if he's doing it that way."

Kali's grin widened. "Mr. Fairways, I am afraid everything you just said flew straight over my head. I'm about as landlubbery as a girl can get!"

"Well, if you could let Brodie know—"

Kali put up a hand. "I'm afraid I'm going to have to stop you there. I am quite certain anything you tell me would be lost in translation. How about you tell him yourself on your way out?"

She watched him consider the idea. Neutral

territory… A way to tease away the groundless fears…

"Oh, I wouldnae want to get in his way or anything."

"You wouldn't be," she assured him. "I think he'd quite like it. Especially since you'd be doing him a double favor."

"How's that, then?"

"Well…" She leaned forward conspiratorially. "So many people don't seem to understand he's been given the all clear as far as his health and his time in Africa are concerned."

"Oh?" Mr. Fairways' fingers twiddled with the end of his handlebar mustache. "Is that right?"

"Absolutely." She crossed her heart and held up two fingers. "Girl Scouts' honor."

"Aye…there was some talk about it at the Eagle and Ram."

Kali checked a broad grin. *That* was where she'd seen him before. The pub!

"Given that you're the mayor of the island—"

"Oh…" Mr. Fairways tutted, a modest smile on his lips. "Only *honorary*, dear. We don't go for too much pomp and ceremony up here."

"Well, even so, it seems to me you have the islanders' respect, so if you were to be seen speaking with Brodie…you know, just giving him a few pointers…it might put a lot of people's minds at ease." She paused while he took in the information. "I've seen Brodie's medical paperwork myself. If you like, I can show you."

"No, dear, no. That won't be necessary. I saw him at his father's funeral. Didn't want to interfere, is all." He pushed himself up to stand. "I think I might head on out and have a word with Brodie now. No need to take up any more of your time."

"It was my pleasure, Mr. Fairways."

He gave her a nod and a smile as he tugged on his overcoat. "You'll do well here, lassie—with a smile like that. And sensible, too. Who knows? We might make an islander of you yet?"

From your lips, Mr. Fairways...

"You take care of yourself, then, Mr. Fairways." Brodie gave a wave as the sprightly fellow headed off down the road toward the pub for his evening pint, flat cap firmly in place.

Would wonders never cease?

Mr. Fairways...standing right out there in the middle of the street...chatting with him about boat mechanics. He'd been the first one to cancel his appointment when Brodie had returned to Dunregan. It had felt like being struck by a battering ram. Only to be hit again and again as one by one his patients had dropped off the appointment list like flies.

Had it been the Ebola or had it been an unofficial mourning period?

It had been easier to blame the nonexistent contagion rather than face up to years of pushing people away. With his father gone, he might have finally succeeded in pushing near enough everyone away.

Except his auntie. Stoic Ailsa. Unflappable at the worst of times. She was the only one who could tease Callum out of the mountains. Something *he* needed to put a bit more energy into, with all this unexpected free time.

"Did you get your advice, then?"

"Kali!" Brodie turned abruptly. "Sorry, I was miles away. What was that?"

"Mr. Fairways was saying something about props or frames—"

"Kali O'Shea…" He took a step toward her. "You didn't have anything to do with Mr. Fairways suddenly turning into a chatterbox, did you?"

"Oh, no. Nothing like that. He was just interested in your project, and I didn't have a clue what he was talking about, so I thought—"

"Kali," Brodie interrupted with a knowing smile, "you are about as transparent as a glass of water."

She grinned, the smile lighting up her eyes. Was that a dimple on her cheek?

"Well, whatever you did or didn't say…thank you." He pulled a tarp over the pile of wood and began to organize his tools into some newly purchased boxes. "I'm not going to hold my breath for everyone to come back tomorrow demanding an appointment with me, though."

"Well, isn't that the mad thing about life? You just never know." She raised her eyebrows and tacked on, "Do you?" for added emphasis.

"I suppose."

If he could get back to work at the clinic then the ticker would start on his promise to his father, he could wipe his hands clean of his past, move on with the future and…and Kali would be gone.

He wasn't quite ready to give her up just yet.

"Don't you worry, Kali. Things work at a glacial pace up here. Besides, what would you do if I were hogging all the patients? Your contract is for a month, and if you weren't busy at the clinic—"

"I'm sure I could think of a load of things to keep me occupied."

"In Dunregan? You must be joking!" Then again…he could think of a number of things to do with Kali to keep her occupied.

Uh…where did that come from?

"Of course Dunregan," Kali replied emphatically, blissfully unaware of his internal monologue.

What would she want with someone who hauled around baggage as oversized as his anyway?

"There's this Polar Bear Club I still have to find out about," Kali continued enthusiastically, "and I've discovered there's no need to go to the tourist office. The patients have told me about so much more. There's the cake-baking club, hiking up in the mountains, fell running—"

"You're a runner?"

Kali nodded, his question jolting her back to another time and place. She'd never give up running. It was her escape.

"Good call." Brodie interrupted her silent musings. "Running is one thing I missed about being here. The mountain tracks are out of this world. Just the views alone are worth the burn."

"Finally!" She forced on a cheery smile. "Something you like about the island."

"Ach…" He waved away her playful gibe. "There's plenty I like about the old lump of rock. Doesn't mean I have to stay here till my bones are creaking, does it?" He gave her a sly grin. "So…given that we've established neither of us are going to be here forever…maybe you and I could go for a run sometime before you go back?"

"That'd be great!" Her smile faltered a bit.

"Or not. If you prefer running alone."

"No, no. A run together would be great."

There was something in her response Brodie couldn't put a finger on. She wanted to stay? She didn't like running with other people? She didn't like being with him? None of the puzzle pieces fit quite right.

She leaned her bicycle on her hip and rubbed

her hands together, blowing on them even though they were kitted out in a new pair of mittens.

"I see you've been to the shops for a bit of warm-weather gear."

"Yes!" She nodded with a self-effacing laugh. "I think I must've spent my entire month's salary on a Dunregan wardrobe, but I'll finally be warm tonight."

"You're joking, right?"

She shook her head.

"Doesn't the heating work where you are?"

"Um…not really. But it's fine. Although my fire-making skills could do with a bit of improvement."

"I could show you. I'm all wrapped up here." Brodie gave the shed a final scan and flicked off the overhead lighting. "Where is it you're staying again?"

"Oh, it's fine. Honestly. It's just a small cottage, and I've got loads of warm clothes now. As long as I wear all of them I'm cozy as a teapot."

"Kali. Which cottage?" he pressed.

"It's fine—honestly."

He wagged a finger at her. "I think you've been in Dunregan long enough to know it doesn't take a man long to figure out every single thing there is to know about a person if he sets his mind to it. I can have a word with your landlord, if you like. Who is it you're renting your cottage from?"

"Seriously…" Her voice went up a notch. "I'm absolutely fine!"

Kali looked anything but fine. There was near panic in her voice, and even through the descending murk of the early evening it was more than apparent that any happiness had drained away from her eyes. A need to protect her overrode his instinct to back away.

"Hey, you're all right," he said gently.

He checked an impulse to pull her in for a hug when her body language all but shouted, *Back off!*

"I'm not trying to pry, Kali. I'm just trying to help you. Make sure you don't freeze to death while you're busy covering my back."

"So which is it, then? I'm covering your back or taking over?"

"Easy there, tiger! What's going on? This isn't just about dodgy heating, is it?"

"Sorry, sorry. It's just been…" Her voice trailed off.

"A long day. I know. A long week. And you've done well." Again he fought an impulse to tug her in for a protective hug.

She grabbed the handlebars of her bicycle. "I'll see you tomorrow, then."

"No, sorry… Kali, I can't let you go back to a house with no heating. Let's get your bike atop the four-by-four, then I'll get you home and we'll build you a fire."

Kali eyed him warily, then shook her head.

"Sorry, I don't mean to make such a fuss." She held her bike out for him to put on top of the four-by-four.

"Too many boyfriends chasing you round London?"

"Something like that."

Even in the dark he saw her lips tighten. There *had* been something. He was sure of that now. Something that made her wary of letting people know where she lived. Letting a *man* know where she lived?

Whatever it was, he wasn't going to pry it out of her tonight. He'd build her a fire and leave her to it. He, of all people, should understand a person's desire to keep things close to their chest.

CHAPTER SIX

"So it's not just me, is it?" Kali was almost pleased to see Brodie struggling as much as she had with getting the fire to light.

No. *Pleased* wasn't the right word. *Relieved* was more like it. Proof she wasn't useless at looking after herself.

Not that it covered over all the fuss she'd made about him knowing where she lived. Behaving like she had only drawn attention to the fact she had something to hide. And the whole point of coming up here had been because it had seemed safe. A place where she could finally stop the relentless need to check over her shoulder.

Years of medical school in Ireland had felt safer...but her mother had an Irish connection. One she had always been terrified her father would investigate. Perhaps the passage of time had softened his anger.

"It appears not, Dr. O'Shea," Brodie replied, leaning back on the heels of his work boots. "I've got a guess as to why it isn't working, though."

"Why's that?"

"This is a summer cottage."

"Why would that mean the fireplace wouldn't work? It's not like summer is tropical up here."

He raised an eyebrow.

"Well, it isn't."

Brodie turned his focus back to the fire. "It could be loads of reasons, but my guess is the top cap was knocked off the chimney and your flue has been stuffed with leaves, or a birds' nest, so you've no longer got a draw. Easy enough to fix, but only with the right tools. We can get Jimmy Crieff to take a look tomorrow, but tonight..." Brodie's tone changed from informational to non-negotiable. "You're coming home with me."

"I'm *sorry*?" she protested, but just as suddenly realized there was a part of her that felt relief. Someone to look after her. And not just anyone. Someone who made her feel safe.

"I'm not going to let you stay here in the freezing cold, am I? What sort of man would I be, leaving you here all alone to catch pneumonia?" He put on a jaunty grin. "Then we'd have to get another locum in to cover for the locum, who is covering for the doctor, who would have to learn how to make chicken soup."

Kali felt herself relaxing. "So would it be a good idea for me to offer to make dinner tonight in thanks?"

"Throw a few things in a bag," Brodie ordered before she could rescind. "I'll get the car warmed up while you get your things together."

She went to her bedroom, a bit astonished at how easy it was to go along with the plan. As if her trust in Brodie was innate. The first person in—years, really. *Years*.

Her mother had been right. *"Have faith,"* she had whispered, pressing some money into Kali's hand before hugging her one last time. "One day you will find a man you love and trust, and your lives together will be *good*."

Kali pressed her eyes shut tight, too late to prevent a couple of tears from popping out. Maybe that was what linked her to Brodie. Two pseudo-orphans, hoping for a safe harbor from all that had passed before.

"You grew up *here*?" Kali could hardly believe her eyes.

Even in the darkness it was easy to see the McClellan family house had a substantial footprint. When Brodie flicked on the lights as they entered what she saw took her breath away.

The design was a stunning combination of modern with a healthy nod of respect to the traditional stone buildings speckled across the island. The house was almost Scandinavian in design, with an equal division of glass, wood and stone. Thick oak beams soared up to the roof, supporting vast floor-to-ceiling windows. The central wall of thick stone gave the house a solid grounding.

While the view wasn't visible now, Kali imagined being in the house, particularly in the summer, would feel like being part of the environment that surrounded it. Wild. Protective. Free.

She was so caught up in absorbing all the details of the house she barely heard Brodie when he answered her.

"I was born in one of the cottages you might've seen on the seafront, near the ferry docks, but when my parents found out my brother was coming along a few years later—he was a surprise—they put an unexpected inheritance toward building this place."

"Tell me about your brother."

The subject brought a light to her eyes that it had never brought to his own.

"The wayward McClellan! Never met a mountain he didn't like." He tried to affect a comic voice to cover up how he really felt. His kid brother—Callum. The brother constantly disappearing off, only to be returned hours later by a friend or a neighbor, twigs in his hair, moss on his jumper, an unapologetic grin on his face. The brother he could have looked out for a whole lot better than he had.

"He sounds interesting."

"He is that," Brodie agreed. And he meant it. "He's on the mountain rescue squad…does test rides for off-road cycle companies all over Europe. First-class nutter."

"He sounds like fun."

That was one way to put it.

"He doesn't live here with you?"

"No. Well…sort of. He comes down when he needs things. A twenty-seven-year-old man trapped in the habits of a teenager. But mostly he stays in his but 'n' ben up in the mountains."

"His *what*?"

"A cottage. It's basically two rooms. One for sleeping in and one for all the rest. Kind of like the one you're staying in, but with a working fireplace and all his mountain bikes. He comes down every now and again to stay. And steal." He jiggled his eyebrows up and down.

Brodie's show of brotherly consternation couldn't mask the obvious love he had for Callum. What Kali wouldn't give for just one day with her sister. To make sure she was safe. Ensure her father's fury hadn't shifted to her when Kali had fled.

She forced herself to focus on the house. Wood. Stone. Glass. Deep-cushioned sofas inviting a person to come in and stay awhile. A huge hide on the flagstones in front of a large open fireplace. Highland cow? It was certainly hairy enough.

"It's so different from all of the other houses here." She lowered her voice, speaking in the hushed tones one used in a church. "It's absolutely beautiful."

"Aye, well…"

Kali giggled. Spell broken. She could see in

Brodie's eyes there was an untold story nestling there amongst the throwaway line. "Is that something all of you Scots say—or just the islanders?"

"I think you'll find it's most Scots. Our rich and varied dialect hard at work! Now, then…" Brodie rubbed his hands together. "Let's get you a room, shall we? And then we'll see about getting something rustled up for tea."

Brodie took Kali on a high-speed tour of the rest of the house. An expansive kitchen, a pantry the size of her flat in Ireland, a cozy snug with a television, and, toward the rear, a more formal sitting room and a huge swirl of a staircase leading up to the bedrooms.

He showed Kali to one of the two guestrooms his parents had had built—styled to make the guests feel like they were in a tree house—and brushed off Kali's compliments, muttering something about seeing her down in the kitchen after she'd had a chance to settle in.

As he walked back down to the kitchen Brodie tried to see the house though Kali's eyes. Time had dulled the memory of just how amazing they'd all thought it was as they'd seen it coming together, stone by beam, by slate. There was no question about its appeal. But it was weighted with just about every single reason he found it hard to stay in Dunregan.

Putting down roots. Family. Commitment. All things he was quite happy to put on hold. Indefinitely. And yet showing Kali around had tapped a pretty deep well of pride…and affection. She had a way of bringing out the positive…and it felt good. Healing.

Kali swooped into the kitchen, layers of clothes peeled off to reveal a simple flowery button-up blouse and a swishy little skirt, her delight still wholly undisguised.

"It's so warm in here!"

"My parents had the house built with underfloor heating. It keeps the place pretty cozy, even in winter."

"You mean spring, right?"

"It might be spring where *you're* from, darlin'—but Dunregan doesn't acknowledge spring for at least another month. If you're lucky."

"No matter how hard you try, you're not going to convince me to see the downside of living here, Brodie."

"An eternal optimist, aren't you?"

It would've been so natural to reach out and tug her in close to him. Snuggle into the nook between her neck and the silky swoosh of hair cascading over her shoulder.

"Something like that." Kali's green eyes flicked away for a second, then back to his. "Did your parents design this place?"

"My mother. She was an architect and this was her third child. Her words, not mine," he added hastily. He might have issues to spare, but no one had begrudged her the passion she'd had for their family home.

"It's really gorgeous."

Brodie stuck his head into the refrigerator, making a show of rifling through the cluster of packets to see what would go together. He could hardly bear to think of all the buildings his mother would have designed if she'd lived.

"Guess I forget to stop and appreciate it," he mumbled from the refrigerator, not believing his own words for a second.

He missed her every single day. Had never understood why his father and brother hadn't turned on him after her death. Logic dictated that squalls were tempestuous things. Sometimes one side of the island would see the crueler side of Mother Nature whilst the other side carried on none the wiser. But he knew she wouldn't have been out there at all if it hadn't been for him.

Being here, living in this house, was a penance of sorts. One he'd be doing for the rest of his days, no matter where he was. Being on Dunregan in the family home minus the family just made it more...acute.

He pulled a couple of things out of the refrigerator and followed Kali's gaze.

"She did all this herself?"

"Not entirely. It is the interwoven dreamchild of my architect mother and the beautiful craftsmanship of my never-met-a-tool-I-didn't-like father."

"Did the skill base skip a generation?" Kali teased gently.

"Just a child. Callum got the handy genes," Brodie conceded, a smile playing on his lips as he looked at the house afresh.

Having Kali here gave him an unexpected bolstering of strength. The ability to see his family from a loving perspective rather than one tainted with the guilt and sorrow he'd hauled around all these years. It also brought back the unexpected intimacy he'd felt on That Night at the pub. As if he'd opened another door to himself he would normally have kept locked tight.

What was it he'd felt?

Kismet.

Just as his parents' relationship had been. Predestined. Two like-minded souls bucking staid ways and setting new trends on their beloved Dunregan.

At least his mother had seen the house finished. Lived in it three years with her "flock of boys," as she'd called them all.

And his father! The iron rod of strength in that man was unparalleled. Only heaven knew how he'd done it, but his father had treasured that house, *and* his sons, every hour he'd lived. A testament to his love for his wife and family.

"Right!" Brodie clapped his hands together and

surveyed the pile of food on the kitchen counter for a moment. Enough memory lane. Time to focus on the present. "How do you feel about chicken stroganoff?"

"Never heard of it," Kali replied, accepting the bundle of vegetables Brodie was handing her.

"That's because...we are going to invent it." He flashed her a smile. "If it's really good we could always call it Chicken *à la* O'McClellan?"

What a difference an hour made! Between the music blaring away on the stereo, the food sizzling on the stove-top and the quips they were slinging at each other, Kali felt as if she'd entered an alternative universe. Or maybe the house was enchanted. Being here with Brodie felt like... *home.*

She tried to squelch the thought instantly, for fear of jinxing it.

"Turn it up!" Brodie called from across the broad flagstone kitchen.

"I just did!" she shouted above the already-blaring pop tune.

"Even more! I *love* this song!" he called, hands either side of his mouth, his voice barely audible above the volume. *"Let's dance!"*

He jumped and twisted his way into the middle of the room and let loose. Arms flying in the air, hair taking flight with his accelerated movements, his face a picture of pure abandon.

Kali didn't need to be asked twice. How often had she let herself just...*be*.

She started slowly at first. Hips taking on the beat of the music, eyes closing as she let her practical self float away while her body tuned in to the rhythm. She began to lose track of time and place. It was an old pop song. One that had been popular when she was a teenager, living at home with her mum, dad and sister. When trust had been a given and fear something other people felt. It said nothing but *happy* to her.

She raised her hands above her head and began to twirl as her arms took on a life of their own— obeying nothing but the rhythm of the song as it filled her, from head to toe, with joy.

When she opened her eyes she felt Brodie's eyes on her in an instant. There was a look in them she hadn't seen before and she let herself be drawn in by the magnetism of the bright blue. They danced and whooped and by some sort of silent agreement their movements became more synchronized. The sway of their hips matched each other's, their breath was coming in deep, energized huffs.

And then without either of them seeming to notice the music changed. Their movements changed with it. Slow, sensual, instinctive. Brodie was close now. Incredibly close. She looked up into his face, felt their shoulders still gently swaying back and forth, back and forth, in a cadence that almost demanded intimacy.

He slipped his broad hands onto her hips and tugged her in, closer to him. "May I have this dance?"

His eyes were a bright blue, lit up by an accelerated heart rate and—she was sure of it now—a mutual attraction.

A shower of untethered electricity lit up parts of Kali she hadn't known existed. Her breasts were hyperaware of the satin and lace of her bra. The soft swoosh of skin just below her belly button could feel where the lace lining of her panties shifted and smoothed against her skin—almost as if Brodie was tracing his finger just out of reach of her most sensitive areas.

She felt one of his hands slide up her back as the other sought to weave his fingers through hers, then held her close enough to his chest that she could feel his heart beat.

Everything about the moment felt forbidden. And inevitable. She could feel her hair shifting back and forth along her shoulders as Brodie's hand swept down her back to her waist. The shift of his fingers over the curves between her breasts and hip elicited hypersensitive tingles, as if she were being lit up from within.

If she had thought she knew what being touched by a man was like before, she knew for certain she had had no idea until now. Each infinitesimal movement of Brodie's fingertips, hips, even his breath spoke to her very essence.

He untangled their fingers and tipped her chin up as he lowered his lips to meet hers. Tentative at first. A near-chaste kiss. Then another. Longer, more inquisitive. His short beard was unbelievably soft. Kali's fingers crept up to trace along his jawline as his hands cupped hers. Her lips parted, wanting more than anything to taste and explore his full lips.

A soft moan passed between the pair of them—she had no idea where it had started or how it had finished—she was only capable of surrendering to the onslaught of sensations: on her skin, inside her belly, shifting and warming, further, deeper than she'd ever experienced. She felt delicate and protected in his arms. And utterly free to abandon herself to the erotic washes of heat and desire coursing through to her very core.

Already her lips were feeling swollen. In one swift move she felt Brodie tuck his hands under her buttocks, pull her up to his waist and swing her round to the countertop. She couldn't help it. She tipped her head back and out came a throaty, rich laugh she hardly recognized as her own.

Brodie nuzzled into her exposed neck, kissing the length of it with the periodic flicker and tease of a nibble or lick. Kali felt empowered to give herself up to nothing other than feeling and responding, touching and being touched.

Brodie's fingers teased at the hem of her jumper, shifting past her singlet and touching bare skin. Never before had she understood the power of a single caress.

As his hands slipped along her waist and on to her back she wove her fingers through his thick blond hair, tiny whimpers of pleasure escaping her throat as his thumbs skidded along the sides of her breasts.

"Are you okay with this?" Brodie's voice was hoarse with emotion.

"Very," she managed. And she meant it. This was entirely mutual.

He cupped her chin in one of his hands and drew a long, searching kiss from her.

"Want to see the room I grew up in?"

She managed a nod, her brain all but short-circuiting with desire.

Brodie took her hand as she jumped off the countertop and, laughing, she reached out to turn off the stove with the other. Dinner could wait.

Dinner would have to wait.

Giggling like a couple of teenagers, they ran up the stairs. The music shifted as they took the steps in twos, this time to a gentle male voice lazily singing along to the simple melody of a guitar.

"You're sure you're sure?" Brodie looked over

his shoulder as they hit the landing. "It won't be weird for you or anything? Working together?"

"If we'd listed all the things that are weird about this we probably wouldn't have kissed in the first place," Kali replied, more for her own reassurance than Brodie's.

"That, my lovely, is a very good point." He pulled her in close to him for another long, deeply intentioned kiss.

My lovely.

The words trilled down her spine. She couldn't remember a single time when she'd been called lovely before. She'd had the odd med school romance, but nothing had stuck. No one had brought her to life in the way Brodie had. And for the next few hours at least she was his—all his. Gladly. Willingly. *By choice.*

And it felt amazing.

Kissing and touching and exploring, and with a frantic dispensing of winter clothes, they eventually made their way to a doorway flung open with grand finesse by Brodie, before he hooked a hand onto her thigh and tugged her legs up and around his waist again.

"Mind your head," he cautioned—unnecessarily, as she'd lowered her lips to taste his yet again.

There was only a deep purple singlet and a lace-edged bra between them. Brodie's shirt had disappeared somewhere between the bottom of the stairs and the top, and his body heat was beginning to transmit directly to Kali, stoking her hunger for more.

"What if I were to throw you on the bed and have my wicked way with you?" Brodie pulled back, eyes crackling with anticipation.

"Go on, then," she dared him, hardly believing the words were coming out of her own mouth as she spoke. "Finish what you started."

More tigress than tabby was right.

The sexual tension igniting between the pair of them was the most intense thing Brodie had ever felt with a woman. He loved holding Kali's petite body, feeling the weight of her thick hair on his hands as he spread his fingers across her back. If he'd ever thought her timorous, he was being set straight now. This was alpha with alpha. Each using their personal advantages to bring the other pleasure.

He took one hand and shifted it lower, to cup one of her buttocks, and then half threw, half laid her upon his bed. Seeing her stretching to her full length as she hit the deep blue of his duvet, he felt another surge of desire.

"Protection?" she asked softly, pulling her ebony hair into one hand and twisting it into a spiral.

He stood, mesmerized, like a man who was seeing a goddess for the very first time. She looked up at him, eyes heavy lidded and sexier than ever. *Definitely more tigress than tabby.* With a fluid whoosh of her hands she fanned her hair out across her shoulders.

"On it." He turned to check his chest of drawers, then whipped around. "Don't move…I want you to stay exactly as you are."

Kali blinked once, as if processing the thought, and then again, as though she'd made her decision. "What are you waiting for?"

Socks flew everywhere as Brodie searched the top drawer for the little foil packets he vaguely remembered putting in there after he'd cut yet another relationship short. All he could think of right now was Kali, and giving her the most pleasure a woman could have. His fingers struck gold and he turned round with a flourish.

Her beauty near enough sucker punched him. He was the moth and she was the flame. Her fingers were teasing at the spaghetti straps of her singlet.

"Stay still," he whispered, easing himself onto the bed beside her.

He wanted to be the one to slip the fabric up and over her head. To tease the hooks away from her bra, freeing her breasts to his touch, his kisses. He wanted to give her a night of undiluted pleasure.

Kali obliterated his moment's hesitation as she wriggled close to him, rucking up the soft fabric of her top as she moved. Skin against skin. Lips exploring. The tip of her tongue slowly circling the dark circle of his nipple. Her fingers and his fought with his belt buckle and won. Each move, each discovery, only increased Brodie's desire to be with her. Tenderly. Passionately.

He rolled on top after yanking his trousers off, his forearms holding part of his weight above her soft-as-silk body as he sought her eyes for permission to continue. There was no question now of how much he wanted her. She must feel it, too, as she pressed and shifted against the length of his erection.

A nod and a smile were all he needed. And exactly what he received.

Slowly. He would take his time. This was a woman worth taking his time over, and he wasn't going to risk missing a single square inch of Kali O'Shea.

CHAPTER SEVEN

CONTENT DIDN'T EVEN begin to cover how Kali felt. This was the sixth…no, the seventh day she and Brodie had decided her place was too cold to stay in and she had accidentally on purpose ended up in his bed. Sure, they were both being a little coy about it during "office hours"—but here in bed? *Mmm...* A whole new world of trust and intimacy had woven its invisible threads, linking them in a way she hadn't imagined possible.

She stretched like a cat, reveling in the contrast of her skin against Brodie's body. She felt soft and pliable whilst he… *Whoo!* He was all muscle and strength. A spray of fireworks went off in her belly when she remembered their night together. If she had a trophy, she'd hand it to Brodie for his skills in the art of lovemaking. She had never, ever, in her limited romantic history, felt as amazing as she had with the man who had protectively held her in his arms all night long.

"Is that you up?" Brodie murmured.

She pushed herself up on her elbows and gave his cheek a kiss.

"Yup! Rise and shine—we've got another big day of work ahead of us!"

"Already?" Brodie put his arm around her

shoulder and tugged her back in to nestle alongside him.

*Sweet monarch of the glen, that man smells
good!*

"Guess we'd better get you fed and watered,
then," he murmured after a few minutes.

"What? Like a horse?" She whinnied and asked
for coffee in her best horse voice.

"Is that how you win everyone over?" he intoned.

"Something like that. You should hear my duck
voice."

"Go on, then."

She asked for toast with butter in her duck
voice. She'd used it countless times to entertain
her little sister when she'd been in the toddler in-
defatigable *"Again!"* phase.

Kali fought with the sobering fact that her sister would be a young woman now. Completely
changed.

The shard of reality all but shattered the undiluted joy she'd been feeling over the past week.
Nights of old-fashioned fun and frisson with just
about the most gorgeous man she'd ever laid eyes
on.

Okay, fine. *The* most gorgeous man she'd ever
laid eyes on.

"Impressive." Brodie pulled himself up to sit,
making sure a pillow was tucked beneath her head
as he did so. "I'll give you a pound for every pa-

tient you see using only that voice." His light tone showed he was oblivious to her shift of mood.

Live in the moment, Kali. It's the only thing you have in your power.

"I think I'll use my Dr. O'Shea voice and save all my other voices for you."

"Well, that's very generous." He popped a kiss on her forehead. "So many hidden talents, Kali! I wonder what other hidden treasures I'll uncover over the next two weeks."

"Two?" she squeaked. *Was that it?*

"Just under, actually." He frowned. "Not so long now, my little whip-poor-will."

Kali bit into the inside of her cheek. There it was again. The reminder that she wasn't staying. She turned away from Brodie, snuggling into the warmth of his embrace so he couldn't see the complex emotional maze she was navigating. It seemed absolutely mad…but a mere fortnight here on Dunregan with Brodie and she felt the safest and happiest she had since she'd left the family home all those years ago.

It was the first time she'd felt whole. As if Kali O'Shea was a real person and not a name she'd had to invent so she could never be found by her father and the man he'd arranged for her to marry.

Brodie made a contented *mmm*…noise and tugged her in closer. It was almost ridiculous how good she felt with him. A crazy thought entered her head. She knew that if in some mad turn of events Brodie were to ask her to stay, she would say yes.

Her gut, heart, the *tips of her toes* were telling her that this feeling she was experiencing right now—this deep, instinctive peace she was feeling—was the elusive "it" she'd heard so much about when people spoke of love.

Which, of course, was utter madness.

Particularly given the fact they'd all but been living in a self-contained lust cocoon, all safe and cozy, tucked away from the world and all its problems. Problems just waiting to be dealt with...

She heaved a silent sigh, turned around to face Brodie. His eyes opened just enough to give her a flash of their cornflower-blue brightness before shutting with heavy-lidded contentment. She traced a finger along his cheekbone and bounced it to his lips. Eyes still closed, he gave her fingertip a kiss. A kiss she transferred to her own lips with a smile. He rolled over to face the window and she cuddled into him for a cozy spooning. His body and her body matching with a made-in-heaven perfection.

It was probably just as well she only had a couple of weeks left on Dunregan. Getting too attached would only mean lying to this gorgeous man beside her. There was no way she was going to burden him with the complexities of her past. The family she'd been forced to leave behind. The father who had irrevocably betrayed her trust.

Brodie abruptly flung the duvet to the side, as if cued by the universe to remind her how fleeting their time together was.

Only two more weeks.

He leaped out of bed and she rolled into the warm spot he'd left behind as he stood at the windows, facing the expansive sea view.

"Is that snow?"

"Oh, my gosh!" Kali scrambled out of bed, pulling on Brodie's discarded rugby jersey, and joined him, expertly stuffing the dark thoughts to the back of her mind.

Outside the window, big fat flakes were floating down from a gray sky completely unencumbered, ultimately finding purchase on a bit of slate, the deep green tines of a fir tree, or the dock she could see stretching out to the edge of the bay the house had been built on. It would take some time for a thick blanket of snow to build up—but the still beauty of the scene took her breath away.

"How beautiful…"

"Always see the bright side of things—don't you, my little Miss Sunshine?"

If only you knew!

"It's mesmerizing to watch."

"And dangerous."

"*You* always see the dark side of things, don't you, Mr. McGloomy?" Her lips twitched.

Brodie held her gaze as if daring her to break

character. Soon enough her lips broadened into a wide smile.

"I suppose so. But with you here…" He tugged her close, wrapping his arms around her so that they both faced the wintry scene. "It's impossible not to see what's right with the world."

If she could preserve this moment in time she would.

Together they stood, enjoying the wintry scene, before a clock somewhere down on the ground floor bonged out the fact that it was high time for them to get ready for work.

"Back to reality?" Kali quipped—not really minding a jot. If this could be her everyday reality she would take it in an instant.

"Right, my beauty. We'd best get a move on." Brodie dropped a kiss on top of Kali's head. "All those sick people for you to see, and I've got to figure out how on earth to build a boat."

"I'm sure there's a video on the internet," Kali teased, disappearing into the bathroom.

She stopped when the reflection of a woman caught her eye in the mirror. A happy, tousle-haired woman, her lips peeled apart in a wide smile.

It was, she realized with a start, herself. The woman she never thought she'd have a chance to be. Plain ol' happy.

"That's an interesting approach."

"Johnny! I didn't see you there."

Brodie put down the sander and wiped his brow with his forearm before shaking hands with his old classmate. It might have been snowing all morning, but he was feeling the satisfying warmth that came from physical labor.

"I was just going to clamp the…uh…the sheer clamp to the front bit. The bow."

"You've not really got a clue, have you, Brodie McClellan?" Johnny asked with a friendly guffaw. "I've built nine of these skiffs since you took yourself off to get your fancy medical degree, and I can spot a man who doesn't have the first idea how to put together a boat from a mile off. Had to run up here from the docks to set you straight."

"Why'd you have to build so many? None of them watertight enough to float?" Brodie gibed back.

He'd missed this. Just being able to blether with his schoolmates. The folk who knew him best. Although Kali was coming up a very close second…

"All of them, you cheeky so and so," Johnny mocked, quickly starting the one-two, one-two fist jabs of a man ready to clock another one in the jaw.

"So, are you going to stand there waiting for a fight that's not going to help, or are you going to help me?"

Brodie handed him a clamp. Not that he knew if it would be useful, but it was to hand.

"I'm guessing they didn't teach you anything useful like shipbuilding down at your medical school, then?" Johnny teased the clamp expertly into place and put together two bits of the boat Brodie had thought would forever remain apart.

"Right before the diseases of the liver lecture," answered Brodie with a grin.

Johnny ran a practiced hand along the golden grain of the planks and started reorganizing them into a more recognizable pattern. A boat shape.

"So, it's looking like your trip to Africa didn't kill you, then," he said, after a few moments of turning Brodie's "workshop" into something that actually *looked* like a workshop.

"Nope. You're stuck with me."

Johnny looked up from the woodpile, mouth agape. "For good? You've moved back to the island?"

Brodie's gut instinct was to laugh facetiously. But the hint of hope in his friend's eyes made him check himself. Johnny was a through and through islander. And, truthfully, the idea of staying, whilst not exactly growing on him, was distinctly more appealing than it had been a few weeks ago.

"You've definitely got me here for the foreseeable future." Brodie chose his words tactically. He still had an out if he wanted one.

"That's good to hear." Johnny nodded his approval. "We always thought you'd bugger off to some exotic country for good once your dad passed."

"We?"

"Helen and I. You remember Helen from school?"

"Of course I do! Seared into my brain, the lot of you." Brodie mimed branding his brain. "Looks like she's keeping you well fed."

"Aye, that'd be about right." Johnny patted his gut appreciatively. "Her steak bridies won me over years ago. I can't get enough of them. It's what inspired her to start the bakery. She makes a mountain of them every Hogmanay, remember?"

"I don't think I've been to yours on New Year. Not since you shacked up with Helen anyway."

"Hey, that's my wife you're talking about. I made an honest woman of her."

"Well, congratulations to you both! Belated, they may be, but no less heartfelt." Brodie shook his friend's hand, genuinely happy for him.

"No one's made you bend *your* knee, then?"

"No," Brodie answered quickly. Too quickly. He'd been too busy trying to outrun his past ever to think about starting a future. A flash of Kali lying in his bed, hair fanned out on the pillow, came to him. If he were the type to settle down...

Johnny examined the wood again, giving it another once-over with hands that had known more than their share of physical labor. "We reckoned none of us were good enough for you—

that's why you had to go off seeking your fortune elsewhere."

Brodie shook his head. "No, that's not even remotely true, Johnny. I'm just—" He looked up to the dark skies, still ripe with snowfall, and sought the right words. "I suppose I just wanted to see what the world had to offer."

"And now, like a wise man, you've come back to Dunregan. The home of Western civilization!"

They laughed together, their eyes taking in the tiny village hardly a stone's throw from the clinic. Butcher, baker and a newsagent/post office/coffee shop on one side. Pub, grocery and a charity shop supporting the Lifeboat Foundation on the other. And, of course, the Dunregan Bakehouse. What more did a village need?

"What's the wee girl like? The locum you've got in for all the folk who still think you've got the touch of death about you?"

"Ha! You never minced words, did you, Johnny? Kali? She's fine. Great, in fact."

In more ways than one.

Memories of their nights together were very likely the reason why he had made next to no progress on his skiff. Since when had he become a daydreamer?

"Well, I guess I'll find out in a minute."

"Everything all right?"

Johnny nodded. "Just a wellness checkup for my diabetes. It's pretty much under control now, but Helen always badgers me into coming for these annual checkups."

He gave a *women, eh* harrumph, and turned toward the clinic.

"Good to see you, Brodie. Perhaps we'll catch up at the pub one of these nights, eh? And I'll come along and lend you a hand on that boat of yours later this afternoon, if you're still here. Make sure you don't sink when you put her out to sea."

Johnny winced the moment the words were out of his mouth.

"Oh, mate, I'm *so* sorry—I didn't mean—"

For the first time in he didn't know how long, Brodie took the joke at face value. It *wasn't* a dig about his mother and the dark course their sailing trip had taken.

"Not to worry. I could do with your wise counsel. It's an excellent idea." And he meant it. "See you soon?"

"Soon." Johnny nodded affirmatively.

They shook hands again and Brodie watched him disappear into the clinic.

It was good of Johnny to stop by and have a word. He'd been so engrossed in his sanding he wouldn't have noticed if his old school pal had walked straight on by. But that wasn't the Dunregan way. You saw someone you knew—you stopped and you chatted. People looked after each other as they had done in small communities like this from the dawn of time. Tribal.

He watched his breath cloud and disperse as he huffed out a laugh. He would bet any amount of money this was the type of moment his father had been hoping he would have when he'd made him promise to stay. Clever sod. It was easy enough to stay at arm's length from the people he'd grown up with when he was thousands of miles away. But receiving offers of help on a boat he didn't have a clue how to build…? That was humbling. And it was starting to tease away at the very solid line he'd drawn between himself and those who'd chosen to stay.

He felt his phone vibrate in his pocket before the ring sounded. He tugged it out and took a look at the screen, eyes widening when he saw who it was.

"Callum?" He stepped out of the shed, moving his eyes up to the mountains as if he could see his brother. "What's going on?"

"There's been a wreck."

"What kind of wreck?" Brodie felt his heart rate surge. Was his brother all right?

"I'm fine," Callum said, as if reading his mind. "But you better get up here—with help if you can—the Taywell Pass road."

"What's happened?"

"The snow's right thick up here and a lorry towing a huge load of logs has jackknifed, taking out two oncoming cars as he went. One's flipped and the other is on the edge of a wee loch. Get the fire brigade up as well. We'll need the Jaws of Life. And make sure you've got tow ropes in your four-by-four."

"Do you have your medical kit on you?"

"Only the small bag. I was taking a new bike for a ride down the mountain in the snow."

"Have you got your four-by-four? We can put patients in it if necessary."

"No, just the bike."

Brodie heard his brother give a sharp gasp.

"Callum, are you all right?"

"Fine. Quit your fussing and get up here."

Brodie headed toward the rear entrance of the clinic.

"Right. Ten, twenty minutes max—I'll be there with reinforcements."

"Make it fast, Brodie. The truck driver's in a bad way. Probably internal bleeding. And there's a wee laddie trapped in one of the cars as well."

"Did you ring the air ambulance?"

"Not yet. I wanted to find out your ETA."

"Give them a ring. At least as a heads up."

"Aye—just get a move on, Brodie."

He didn't need telling twice. His brother had said he was fine, but there was something off in his tone.

Brodie hung up the phone and yanked open the clinic door. In a matter of moments he'd got

Caitlyn to cancel the rest of Kali's appointments, put Ailsa in charge of ringing the volunteer fire brigade and coordinating with the ferry captain in case they needed to hold the ship for patients needing hospital care.

He grabbed his own portable medical kit and loaded a couple backboards and everything else he thought would be useful in the cab of his vehicle.

"Where do you want me?"

Kali appeared at the back of the clinic, her new winter coat zipped right up to her chin.

"Passenger seat for now. We can fold down the seats in the back if we need to transport anyone."

"Is there not an ambulance?"

"You're looking at it." Brodie pulled a blue light attached to a wire out of his glove box and clamped it to the top of his four-by-four.

"Brodie?" Johnny stuck his head out through the back door of the clinic. "I hear you're wanting the fire brigade?"

"Aye." Brodie jumped into the four-by-four. "That's me."

"What happened to Davie Henshall?"

"Retired, pal. See you up there as soon as I get a couple of the other lads together. Won't be long."

He waved them off and disappeared back into the clinic, only to be quickly replaced by Ailsa running to Kali's side of the car.

"Here you are, dear." She handed over three flasks. "Hot water if you need it. There's tea bags and sugar and things in the glove box."

"Thanks, Ailsa." Brodie leaned across Kali whilst shifting the car into gear. "We'll give you an update when we get there."

As he hit the road, driving safely but with intent, Brodie could feel his suspicions increase. The call from his brother ran in his head on a loop, refusing to offer up any clues. He would've told him if something was wrong. Wouldn't he...?

Even to think of suffering another loss constricted his throat. That was what this island did. Take and take and take.

He swore softly under his breath.

Stop thinking like a petulant teenager. Life's not perfect anywhere and Dunregan's no different. It's the home your parents loved as much as they loved each other. And you. You're alive. Practicing medicine, which you love. There's a beautiful woman sitting right next to you who could light up your life for the rest of your days if you let her. Now, go find your brother.

Concentrating didn't begin to describe how deep in thought Brodie looked. He was navigating the snow-covered roads with the dexterity of someone who could've walked the island blindfolded. The landscape seemed a part of him. Even more so right now.

"You all right?" Kali finally broke through the deepening silence in the car.

"Fine. We'll be there in just a couple of minutes. I was just trying to work through how we'll sort everyone."

"Triage, you mean?"

"Yes."

"You must be used to this sort of thing with all of the work you've done out in the field. With Doctors Without Borders."

"Mmm-hmm."

Brodie wasn't giving anything away. She wasn't going to lower herself by getting insecure, but this Brodie was an entirely different one from the sexy man who'd pinned her against the wall in the supplies cupboard earlier that morning for a see-you-at-lunchtime snog. Maybe this was Work Brodie, and she was confusing his refusal to engage in conversation with his concentration over what was to come.

She glanced across at him. Jawline tight. Eyes trained on the road. No guesses as to what was going on in his head.

"This'll be my first accident," Kali said.

Brodie shot her a sharp look.

"Outside a clinic or a hospital, I mean," she quickly qualified.

"You'll be fine. A bit less equipment and no nurses to fetch things, but with the help of the fire crew—they've all got basic paramedic skills—you'll be fine."

He shot her another look, one exhibiting a bit more of the Brodie she knew off duty.

He gave her thigh a quick squeeze. "Sorry, Kali. My brother's up in that mess, and he said he was fine but I have a bad feeling."

"In what way?"

"He's trained in mountain rescue—basic paramedic stuff—but he didn't sound like he was doing anything. Normally he would've called while he was doing fifteen things as well as talking to me. One of those rare multitasking males." He gave a weak smile. "Hold up—I think I see them up ahead."

Kali nodded. She got it now.

Family.

The one thing you could never escape. They were woven into your cell structure.

Brodie pulled his four-by-four to an abrupt halt and scanned the scene. Not good. The opposite, in fact. He was out of the cab and crunching across ankle-deep snow toward the stationary vehicles in an instant.

"Callum?" His voice echoed against the hillsides, then was absorbed by the ever-thickening snow.

Kali appeared by his side, all but dwarfed by the large medical kit slung over her shoulder.

"Here." He took a hold of the free strap. "I'll take that. Can you grab the backboards off the roof? *Callum!*" he called again, his tension increasing.

The name reverberated from hillside to hillside, leaving only the hushed silence of snowfall.

He jogged to the logging truck, where there were huge lengths of freshly sawn trees splayed hither and yon, and climbed up to the cab. The driver was slumped over the wheel. Brodie yanked open the door and pressed his fingers to his pulse point. Thready. But he was alive.

"All right there, pal? Can you hear me?"

No answer. The driver's airbag had deployed, bloodying his nose. He could've easily knocked his head on the side window and concussed himself.

"Here's the backboard. Where do you want me?" Kali looked up at him from the roadside.

Brodie used the high step of the cab to scan the site. As his brother had described, there was a car twenty or so meters away at the edge of the loch, and one flipped onto the roadside just a few meters beyond.

He jumped down from the cab.

"Let's do a quick assessment then board up whoever needs it. Get blankets to everyone. *Callum!*"

Nothing.

They ran toward the overturned vehicle and knelt at the windows.

A woman hung, suspended by her seat belt, looking absolutely terrified.

"Madam, are you all right?"

"My boy!" she screamed, hands pressed to the roof of the car. "Can you get my boy out? Billy! Are you all right, darling? Mummy's just here."

"Hello, in there."

Brodie kept his voice calmer than he felt. The accident victims he could deal with. Not hearing from his brother… A sour tang of unease rose in his throat.

He saw the woman trying to release the catch on her seat belt. "I'm Dr. McClellan. We'll help get you and your boy out of the car, but can you keep your seat belt on, please? Don't try to undo it. You could hurt your neck. What's your name?"

"Linda. Linda Brown. Billy—can you hear Mummy?"

Kali tried to pull the rear door open on the driver's side, where a toddler was hanging from his child seat. "I can't get it open!"

"The roof must've been crushed when the car flipped." Brodie gave the door a tug as well, his foot braced against the body of the vehicle. No result. "Can you run down and check the other car while I get these two out?"

The whine of a siren filled the air. The fire department.

"Go on." Brodie waved to Kali to get to the other car while he pulled out his window punch. "Linda, can you cover your face, please? I'm just going to break Billy's window—all right?"

"What about Billy's face?" the panicked mother asked.

"I'll do my best—he should be all right, but we really need to be getting him out."

He held the tool to the window and pressed. The glass shattered but remained intact. Brodie stuck the slim tool into a corner of the window to make a small hole, then tugged as much of the glass away from the boy's face as he could. It fell away in a sheet, exactly where Brodie needed to kneel. He ran over to the backboard and tugged it into place by the window, grabbing his run bag as he did so.

He unzipped his medical kit and raked through the supplies, his fingers finding the neck braces by touch as he tried to find a pulse on the boy's neck.

Yes!

Three out of three so far.

Where the hell was his brother?

"How is he? Is he all right?" called Linda.

"I've got him. He looks good on the outside, but we'll have to wait and see if he's sustained any internal injuries."

Linda began to cry softly, a low stream of "No, no, no…" coming in an unrelenting flow.

Brodie rucked up the boy's shirt. He could see the sharp red marks from the seat belt, but no swelling that would indicate internal bleeding. He'd need tests. X-rays. Everything he didn't have here. The boy needed a proper hospital.

Had Callum called the air ambulance? Could it even fly in this weather? The snow had managed to thicken in the space of ten minutes, shrouding the surrounding mountains and hillsides in cloud.

C'mon, little brother. Throw me a sign you're okay.

"Brodie?"

Johnny appeared by his side, kitted out from head to toe in his all-weather firefighting uniform. Brodie blinked and for an instant saw the young redhead he'd used to play footie with as a youngster. That young lad had been replaced by a man who was ready for action.

"Tell us what you need."

Brodie quickly ran through instructions to get the truck driver out onto a backboard—but not before he'd had a neck brace applied. Then he'd need checks on internal bleeding, heart rate, blood pressure—the usual stats for an extraordinary situation.

"Can you help me get Billy's mother out of the car so we can get the two of them into a warm vehicle?"

"On it, mate."

Brodie looked toward the car by the loch and

couldn't see anyone around it. Where had Kali disappeared to?

He forced himself to be still for a moment, to crush the growing panic. He'd dealt with thousands of people fearing for their lives in Africa. He could do this.

"Brodie?" Johnny tapped his leg. "We've got this if you want to go down to the other car."

"Thanks, pal. I'll do that. Extra blankets and things are in the back of my four-by-four."

Brodie took off at a jog, quickly ratcheting his pace up to a run when the details of the scene became clear. The front of the estate car was completely concertinaed. If anyone was alive in there it would be a miracle. He could hear barking. Dogs in the back? Had to be. There weren't any running around free.

He reached the front of the car, a seventysomething woman inside. The crash's first fatality.

The barking began again in earnest, as if the dogs sensed their owner had been killed. He made a mental note to ring the vet, see if he could come out as well.

He raced to the other side of the car. There was Kali, kneeling next to the mangled remains of a bicycle and...

Oh, no, no, no...

"Callum?"

CHAPTER EIGHT

Brodie dropped to his knees beside Kali, barely taking in the stream of information she was efficiently rattling off. Something about the car beginning to roll into the loch, Callum skidding on his bicycle in an attempt to get it behind the wheel to try and stop it, and not being able to unclip his bicycle shoes from the pedals before the car started rolling. Possible lacerations or puncture. Bones crushed.

His own observations took over as he absorbed the sight of his brother's pale face and contorted torso, only just visible outside the edge of the vehicle. Limited to zero blood flow would be going to his legs. Muscle damage. Tissue damage. Possible paralysis. He'd seen worse. So much worse. But seeing Callum like this sent shock waves of hurt through him. Pain unlike anything he'd ever experienced.

He forced himself to swallow down the emotion before he spoke. "Hey, little brother."

Callum, his head resting on a heat blanket Kali had put under him, tried to crane his neck to see Brodie better, despite the handlebars of his bicycle pinning his chest to the ground.

"Ach, no, Callum. Don't move your head. Why isn't he in a neck brace?" he snapped at Kali.

"He's not complained of any neck pain," Kali replied gently.

He knew the tone. The one he'd used with countless family members of patients. The one that said, *You're missing the big picture, so why don't you take a big breath and—*

"It's his leg, Brodie. I've not administered anything for the pain yet. Until we see what's going on under there it'll be like working in the dark," Kali stated simply. She pulled a phone out of her pocket and wiggled it in his eyeline. "Your Aunt Ailsa's rung your brother's phone here. She couldn't get through to you. An air ambulance is on its way. There is only one that can risk it in this kind of weather."

"How long?" Brodie wished he could take the bite out of his tone, but this was his *brother* they were talking about.

"Ten...maybe fifteen minutes?"

"Right." He cursed up at the sky, then checked his watch. "I suppose they didn't manage to stop the last ferry?"

"No." Kali shook her head, putting up a hand to cut off Brodie's reaction. "But Ailsa rang round and finally got hold of the captain. He's going to drop everyone and come back with a couple of ambulances. Then he'll make the trip back to the mainland."

Brodie nodded, taking in the enormity of the gesture. These were islanders pulling together to help each other. Lives woven together in good and bad. *This*, he suddenly realized, was what island life was about. Being there. Each person doing what they could to enrich and strengthen the vital community.

Brodie gave Kali's hand a quick squeeze. One that he hoped said, *I know I'm being an ass, but help me get through this.* He felt her squeeze back. It was all the sign he needed.

"All right, little brother…let's take a look, eh?"

He shifted to his hands and knees, the snow sending the cold straight through his trousers. But that was nothing compared to what his little brother must be feeling, with half his body trapped underneath that car.

The scene was impossible to break down into simple components. Just a mesh of metal, bicycle wheels, winter clothes and his brother's legs. Everything was indiscernible except the ever-increasing pain on his brother's face.

He shook his head, trying to keep his expression light as he faced his brother. "What have you done, you numpty? Why didn't you say you were in a bit of bother yourself when you rang?"

Brodie tried his best to keep his tone loving. Funny how anger and love wove together so tightly when a person was terrified.

"I wasn't when I rang. I was freewheeling

down the mountainside and saw it all happen. Got down as soon as I could, checked out everyone and then saw Ethel's car going backwards toward the loch."

"Ethel?"

"The woman driving this car." He tried moving an arm to indicate the front of the vehicle, only to cry out in pain. "I—had—to—stop—it—" he panted.

"The world's first human cribbing." Brodie gave him an impressed smile. No need to point out the obvious flaws in the plan.

"I think my bike trail days might be on hold for a while. Always happens when I leave the refrigerator door open." Callum laughed before another wince of pain took over.

Brodie shot a look at Kali. His brother was talking nonsense and—as man-childish as he was—he had never been a babbler.

He gave his brother's arm a rub and felt Callum's body beginning to be consumed by shivering. Could be the cold. Could be shock.

"Kali, have we got a couple more blankets?"

"You bet." She nodded and ran back to the car to retrieve them.

"Callum. How are you feeling, mate? You still with me?"

Callum shut his eyes, but spoke with deliberation. "There weren't any blocks out here, and I wasn't going to let the dogs go into the loch to drown on top of everything..." His voice began to lose what little strength it had.

"You saved them, pal."

He gave his brother's shoulder a gentle squeeze as his eyes traveled the length of his body to his leg, pinned beneath both his cycle and the back wheel of the estate car. Any number of things could be going wrong underneath that mess. If a spoke had jammed into his leg when the car had moved it might easily have pierced a posterior tibial or fibular artery.

"Talk me through what you feel." Brodie's eyes were on his brother.

"Done that." His brother's eyes flicked up in Kali's direction. "Little to no sensation below the knee. Clear of injury other than a strain in the back from such a kickass move!" Callum finished, with a grin that rapidly shape-shifted into a grimace.

"Okay, superhero—we know you're the coolest kid on the block. Any light-headedness?" Brodie's tone was all business.

"Yeah—but there's a blinkin' car on top of me, bro. I'm hardly going to feel great."

"Since when do you talk like one of the boys in the hood?" The words were out before he could stop them.

"Since when did *you* start caring?"

Callum shot. Callum scored.

"Blankets?"

Kali's voice broke through the silence Brodie couldn't fill. Her bustle of action—swiftly wrapping the specialized heat blankets around Callum's torso—was a welcome cover for the surge of guilt threatening to drown Brodie. He was going to get his brother out of this, and he didn't know how but he was also going to make things up to him. Some way. Somehow.

"Kali…" Brodie lowered his voice. "We need to get this car off him."

"Absolutely. But I haven't done a thorough check inside because I saw Callum first. And the car will definitely go into the loch if we pull him out right now. The car could be the only thing holding him together…" Kali countered, not unreasonably.

She was right. If Callum began to bleed out before they had proper medical supplies there, or a means to get him to an operating theater… The very thing that was threatening his life could be keeping him alive.

"Can you get the dogs?"

"What?" Brodie leaned in closer to hear his brother.

"The dogs…in the back of the car."

Callum flicked a familiar pair of blue eyes toward the rear of the vehicle. Sometimes it was like looking in a mirror.

"On it."

Brodie knew his brother would do anything

to help an animal before a human. The man should've been a vet, but that would've meant he had to leave the island for five years' training. And that was never going to happen.

He wouldn't rest easy now unless he knew the dogs were sorted.

The back of the car was undamaged, so the hatch top easily rose when Brodie unlatched it. Two enormous dogs leaped out of the vehicle, one landing with a sharp yelp. A broken leg? Brodie scanned the car for their leashes and easily found them, along with a bag of treats tucked into a side compartment. It was all precious time away from his brother, but Kali was there, assessing and treating him. He trusted her.

He tried unsuccessfully to get the dogs to sit… If the Newfoundlands would just play ball…

"Brodie?"

Kali's voice stopped him in a near-successful attempt at getting the leashes onto the dogs.

"Could you bring the dogs over? Your brother wants to say hello."

"I'm not the ruddy dog whisperer in the family," he grumbled, and only just stopped his eyes from rolling. His brother was in serious trouble here. Time to quit playing the despairing older brother.

One limping, one resisting, Brodie finally managed to get the dogs over to his brother, where they immediately turned into entirely different beasts, licking Callum's face, gently placing their paws on his shoulders as if petting him. These three weren't strangers. They shared a warmer relationship than he did with his own brother, and the hit of shame was hard to shrug off.

But he had to do his best. There was an accident scene to sort. The air ambulance crew would need a situation report when and if they arrived. With the weather closing in they would be lucky. And Linda and her son would need some extra care, not to mention the truck driver. This car needed lifting and towing away from the loch, and the poor soul who was inside needed extracting.

"It's Ethel."

Kali was looking up at him. He shook his head, not understanding.

"Your brother says it's Ethel *Glenn* inside. These are *her* dogs."

His mind raced to connect the dots and in an instant he made the link. Ethel Glenn and her famous shortbread. The long-term widow had stayed up in the croft she and her husband had lived on long after his death some twenty years ago. The villagers went to her, instead of the other way round. She guarded that rickety old croft like an explorer staking a claim on an island full of treasure. Peat and stone. Impossible to make a living on. He'd never understood the draw.

"Brodie?" Johnny jogged over beside them.

"We've got the chap in the lorry boarded up. He's not looking too bad."

The interruption was exactly what Brodie needed to knock him back into action. Working in an emotional daze wasn't going to help any of these people—least of all his brother.

"Anyone keeping an eye on him for cardiac fallback?"

"No, he seems fine."

"If he really got a bash from that airbag—his nose was bleeding, right?"

"Yeah, it's broken. It'll need resetting."

Brodie nodded. "He'll need some scans. If he was within ten inches of that thing when it deployed it won't present now, but we'll want to check for aortic transection, tricuspid valve injuries, cardiac contusions. There's a raft of things that could still go wrong."

"Got it. I'll get one of the lads to keep an eye out. We've got Linda and Billy in our rig, getting warm. Again, nothing obvious—but from what you've said it sounds like they'll be needing a trip to the hospital as well. What now?"

The entire scene crystallized into a series of steps they would need to take as a team. Brodie gave Johnny a grim but grateful smile, then rattled off a list of assignments for everyone, taking on communications with the air ambulances and patient checks for himself. Kali was to con-

tinue monitoring his brother, while the remaining
fire lads prepared the vehicle on top of Callum
for removal.

It couldn't have been more than ten minutes before they all heard the whirr and thwack of the
bright yellow helicopter's rotors as it began its
descent.

Kali had been running on pure adrenaline,
each moment passing with the frame-by-frame
clarity of a slow-motion film—Brodie the confident director, able to shift from patient to casu-
alty to fire crew to dog handler and back again.

It was a blessing that the crash had happened
on the broad stretch of valley where it had, making the helicopter landing possible. Snow, time
and limited visibility were the enemies. Every
person present was a hero, pushing themselves
to the limit to turn a bad situation into something better.

"Where do you want me?" Kali asked when
Brodie appeared on her side of the car.

"Stay where you are. The crew will work
around you." He lowered his voice. "He all right?"

She nodded. Callum's eyes were closed, but
he was resting rather than unconscious. It had to
be tough, seeing your sibling like this. It was exactly why she'd stayed away from her family. To
keep them safe from harm. The violence her father had threatened… She shuddered away from

the fearful thoughts that kept her up at night. She just had to have faith. Faith that her mother and sister were all right.

"We're good," she said with a firm nod.

"You warm enough?" Brodie took a half step forward and drew a finger along her jawline. The distance she'd thought he'd put between them on the way to the crash evaporated entirely.

Times like this prioritized things. She knew that better than most.

She nodded, giving the palm of his hand a soft kiss. The move was totally unlike her, but why the hell not? From the moment she'd stepped off the ferry onto Dunregan she'd felt a change was afoot. She cared for Brodie and she was going to show it. If it backfired then so be it. She'd just have to learn to cope with a whole new level of heartbreak.

Brodie's hand cupped her chin, tipping it up toward him so she could see the gratitude in his eyes. Her heart cinched...then launched into thunderous thumps of relief.

Her instinct had been right.

The intimacy of their moment was snapped in two as the air ambulance doctors jogged toward them with their own backboards and run bags.

On Brodie's signal, the fire department volunteers began preparing the vehicle to be raised and then towed away from Callum and the loch's edge.

"I'll grab hold of the bike," Brodie called as the

noise of the rescue crews increased. "We don't want it yanked away from Callum's leg. If any of the spokes have pierced through we could easily make it worse. Straight up—and only then do you pull the car forward. Got it?"

A chorus of "Aye" and "You got it" filled the air as lines were attached to the mangled front of the vehicle. All the clamps and foot pump lifts were put in place. A hush descended upon the team.

Brodie knelt down by Kali, his fingers automatically shifting to his brother's neck to check for a pulse. She didn't envy him. Not one bit. The intensity of the ache in her heart shocked her, cementing the need to shake it off and focus on Callum.

The car was lifted in seconds, and the cycle went with it, its metal twisted into the undercarriage of the vehicle and—as Brodie had suspected—not one but two spokes had been jammed into his brother's leg. Callum's scream of pain at the release hit the sides of the mountains, pulsing back and forth as each person flew into action.

"All right, let's get him out from under here and onto the scoop stretcher," Brodie called. "Can somebody trench it into the snow so there's not too much movement for him?"

A blur of activity took over. Everyone was acting on well-practiced instinct and skill. Everyone was hiding their dismay at the wreckage that was Callum's leg.

"Compound fractures to the tibia and fibula," one of the doctors said unnecessarily.

"He's got an arterial bleed." Kali jumped forward, pinching the geyser of blood with her gloved hands. "Can I get a clamp?"

"On it," replied one of the air medics, raking through his run bag.

"We're also going to need blood, IV and morphine." She ticked off the list with her other hand.

"Not before splinting him," Brodie interjected. "If you're injecting into the muscle he will feel everything during the splinting."

"Do you have any inhalable diamorphine?" Kali asked the air medic. "He's losing consciousness, so swallowing anything is out of the question."

"Right you are." He handed Kali a clamp and set to mining another part of his bag for supplies.

"Callum? Stay with us, pal. I'm here with you." Brodie held a hand to his brother's face. "Nonresponsive," he muttered, using his other hand to give Callum a brisk sternal rub with his knuckles. "His blood type is A positive. You can give him A positive and negative and O positive and negative. Can we get a defib machine over here?"

"They're using it on the truck driver. He just coded."

Brodie cursed, giving his brother another sternal rub. "C'mon...c'mon! Show me something, here."

Kali flinched in unison with Brodie at Callum's searing scream of pain as they began the messy splinting process. It was a sorry thing to be thankful for—but at least he was alive. The leg was a mess. Months of rehab were in his future. Pins. Bolts. Who knew what other hardware he'd need?

"I'm his brother," Brodie told the crew as they each took a handle of the stretcher and walked as steadily as they could across the frozen ground toward the chopper. "If there's room, I'd like to come along."

"I'll send one of my guys with the two less urgent cases. The mother and child can go on the ferry, so there's room."

"How's the lorry driver? Did he make it through the resus?"

"Only just" was the grim response as they reached the helicopter, where the truck driver was being strapped in. "Definitely something dodgy going on with his heart. He'll need seeing to straight away."

Brodie glanced at his watch, then at Kali. "Will you be taking the ferry as well?"

"Don't you trust my guys?" the head of the aircrew said with a joshing smile.

"Nothing like that, mate. I think I'll just need

to see a friendly face in a couple of hours with the way things are going."

Brodie's eyes locked with Kali's. More passed between them in that single moment than ever had before. The feelings all but tearing her heart in two were shared.

Kali was entirely speechless. What a moment to realize she was in love! Her entire body surged with energy. She felt she was capable of doing anything now that she knew how Brodie felt about her.

"We need to load up!" one of the paramedics called from the helicopter. The rotors were already beginning to swirl into action.

Brodie dug into his pocket and handed her a set of keys, his gloved hand giving hers a quick squeeze. "Go in convoy with the lads from the fire station. They'll help with the transfer to the ambulances. I will try to meet you on the other side. If not—I'll see you at the hospital. Ailsa will meet you at the docks as well, no doubt."

Kali nodded, the to-do list in her head growing, turning into vivid detail and then action.

She ran across to the fire truck, where Linda and Billy were keeping warm, just as the helicopter took its first tentative moves to lift and soon soared off, skidding across the white landscape. She stopped to watch it go, taking away the man she was giving her heart to, having no idea what would happen next.

"Doc?"

Kali whipped around to see Johnny holding the two dogs on leads.

"Are you able to drop these two by the vet's?"

"Yeah, absolutely. Um…" Two big furry faces looked up at her expectantly. They were like small yetis!

"We'll give you a hand loading them up. If you could bring your car here it would save this one's leg an unnecessary journey?"

"Yes, absolutely!" Kali jumped into action—embarrassed to have held them up. "I'll be right behind you in a second."

And right behind you, Brodie, she added silently, with a final glimpse at the helicopter before it completely disappeared from sight.

"I'll come check on you soon, all right?"

Kali waved as Linda and Billy were wheeled off on their gurneys for a full set of scans and X-rays. Bumps and bruises were a definite. She held up a set of crossed fingers that there wasn't going to be anything else.

"Can we get you anything, Dr. O'Shea? A coffee or tea? I think you might be stuck on the mainland tonight."

The charge nurse was halfway out of her station before Kali's brain kicked back into action. The long day was beginning to show.

"No, I'm good, thanks. Just directions to where

I might find another one of the patients who came in on the air ambulance."

"Reggie Firle?"

"No." Kali shook her head. "He was the lorry driver. He's all right, though?"

Best not let the heady combination of lust and love cloud her priorities. Patients. They were number one right now.

"Yes, he's fine. In Recovery, where they are monitoring his heart. So it's…" She ran her finger along the patient list.

"Callum McClellan."

"Oh, yes!" The nurse's finger hit the name at the same time as she spoke. "The one with the doctor brother."

The extremely gorgeous doctor brother, whose existence is eating all of my brain particles.

"Yes."

A more politic answer, she thought, given the circumstances.

Turned out the hour-long ferry ride had given her *way* too much time to think…overthink…and then to worry. Was she thinking she was in love too soon? Reading far too much into *that look*?

She sucked in a deep breath. It was *carpe diem* time.

She nodded and smiled as the nurse gave her directions to the surgical department, where Callum was currently undergoing the first of several surgeries. Her breath caught in her throat. Poor guy. Doing his best to save the dogs, the car, dear old Ethel's remains and now—courtesy of a bicycle shoe—compromising his own future. His life.

The relief Brodie felt when he saw Kali walk into the surgery unit threatened to engulf him. Weighted to the chair he'd only just sat down in, he finally felt able to succumb to the emotions he'd been struggling to keep at bay. He was raw. More so than he'd ever been. And the thought of letting someone see him this exposed was terrifying.

One look at Kali and he knew he shouldn't have worried. The soft smile, the compassion in her eyes, the outstretched arms all said, *You won't have to go through this alone.* As she wordlessly came to him he tugged her in between his knees, his arms urgently encircling her waist when she pulled his head close to her and hit after hit of untethered emotion finally released.

"Want your coffee straight up or with a splash of artery-hardener?" Kali held the small pitcher of cream aloft, poised to pour.

"With a dram of whiskey, but that's a no-goer," Brodie replied, his eyes searching just a little hopefully round the deserted hospital canteen for a bar. Kali's ever-present optimism must be catching.

"Artery-hardener and some not very appetizing

biscuits it is, then, sir!" She handed him a paper cup, with cream still whirling its way through the steaming liquid, and wiggled a packet of vending machine ginger biscuits in front of him that looked as though they could have been made in the last century.

"The middle of the night seems to have its advantages round here."

He put his arm round her shoulder, biscuits and coffee held aloft in his other hand. Being close to Kali was healing. Touching her was downright curative.

"How's that?" She smiled up at him with an *oops* shrug after losing half of her biscuit in a too-deep dunk.

"Lots of sofas to commandeer."

He steered her toward a dimly lit corner of a waiting room not too far from surgery and sank into the well-worn cushions. The stories they could tell...

"I used to dream of working in a place like this."

"Oh, yeah?"

"Well," he qualified, "not exactly like *this*. Inner city. Busy. Never-get-a-moment's-rest busy."

"I thought you preferred international work?" She toed off her thick-tread boots and tucked her feet up underneath her.

"I really love it. Doctors Without Borders does

amazing work. But the idea of being part of a city I know and helping people there—being part of something..."

"Like being part of the community on Dunregan?"

"Touché!" He raised his coffee cup and took a noisy slurp, because he knew it sent a shiver down her spine. But she was right. "This sort of thing does put a lot in perspective."

"Gives you different priorities?"

She wasn't asking. She was telling.

"That sounds like the voice of experience."

Kali's green eyes flicked up to the ceiling, then did a whirl round the room. "Suffice it to say when the unexpected happens for me it all boils down to family."

"The family you never talk about?" He was feeling too worn by the day's events to mince words.

She shook off his question and put one of her small hands on his cheek. He pressed into as she said, softly but deliberately, "Today is about you and your family."

Brodie put his coffee down. Another wave of emotion was hitting him and there would be spillage. Literal and figurative.

"I—I could've done so much more..."

"What do you mean? You did everything you could today."

"Not today. His whole life!" He scrubbed both

hands through his hair. "*I'm* the reason he didn't grow up with a mother, and then I couldn't even stick around to be a big brother for him. I just let him go feral. What kind of a person does that?"

Kali let the words percolate and settle before softly replying, "The kind who hasn't forgiven himself for something that isn't his fault?"

"But it *is*! Was…" He still couldn't believe she wasn't able to see why the blame lay solidly at his feet. He'd *begged* his mother to go out with him that day.

Kali pulled back and folded her hands in her lap, her index finger tapping furiously, the rest of her completely still.

"The only thing you can change," she said at last, "is the future. That is completely in your control."

"Who turned *you* into a sage little Buddha?" He nudged her knee with his own.

"Ohhhh…"

Her lips pressed together and did that little wiggle that never failed to make him smile.

"Let's just say life's had a way of regularly shoving me into the Valuable Lesson department." She tipped her head onto his shoulder.

"Oh, yeah?" He wove his fingers through hers and leaned his head lightly on top of her silky black hair. "What's today's valuable lesson, then?"

"Sticking together," she said without a moment's hesitation. "Through thick and thin."

"This being the thin?"

He could feel her head nod under his.

"This being the thin."

They both stared blankly out into the room. The beeps and murmurings from the wards were more of a white noise than a frenetic addition to the chaos of the day. Callum's surgery shouldn't take too much longer. Then they'd have a much better idea of what lay ahead of him.

Brodie's thumb shifted across Kali's and he took a fortifying inhalation of her wild-flower-and-honey-scented skin.

A sudden hit of clarity came to him. He stayed stock-still for risk of shaking the perfection of it away. Kali was right. He *was* in charge of his future—and she, he knew in his heart, was the missing piece of the puzzle.

"Kali? Have you got anything booked after this gig? The locum post on Dunregan?"

"Not yet."

"Would you consider staying?"

He felt her sharp intake of breath before he heard it.

"You mean at the clinic?" Her voice was higher than usual.

He kept his eyes trained on the double doors of the surgical ward, but continued.

"At the clinic, yes. I don't know how long I'm going to need to be here at the hospital, but..." This was the hard part. The part that scared him silly. "Would you stay with me? Give up your igloo of a cottage? Come stay with me? At home?"

Okay—so it was a little open-ended. It was no proposal, but...

Her fingers, so tiny in amongst his own, squeezed his tightly. But she didn't say a word.

"It's not much of an offer, is it? Stay with a messed-up guy, with a messed-up brother, on an island with a whole lot of messed-up history to untangle."

He laughed. Life had finally pinned him into a corner, forcing him to deal with everything head-on—and, oh, he wished Kali would stay here by his side. He knew he'd have to do the fighting on his own, but knowing that she'd be there waiting for him... He felt his heart skip a beat. Was this how deeply his father had felt for his mother?

"Kali," he said quickly, before she could answer, "I'm not sure what I'm offering you, but... please don't go."

He turned, pressed his lips softly to hers, words suddenly too flimsy for what he needed to communicate. She returned the kiss. Gently...silently.

They sat there for a moment, forehead to forehead, the world around them dissolving into a blur of white noise and shadows. He felt closer to her now than he had when they had made love. Those intimate moments they'd shared? Sheer beauty. But right now…? This…this was the stuff true love was made of.

"Yes," she finally whispered. "I'll be here for you as long as you need me."

CHAPTER NINE

Missing you.
Can't wait to see your beautiful eyes again.
Just dreamed of holding you in my arms.

KALI GAVE A loved-up sigh, forcing herself to put her mobile phone down. She and Brodie had been texting like moonstruck teens since she'd left the mainland three days ago. In spite of all the difficult moments they'd shared at the hospital, these messages were like little drops of heaven.

Ailsa knocked on her office door frame, mugs of tea in hand. "How many are you up to now? I heard Caitlyn put another call through a few minutes ago."

"I can't believe there hasn't been a nationwide alert!" Kali looked at her growing list of volunteers.

"You don't need an alarm system here on Dunregan. Telephones and a trip down to the Eagle for a pint do the trick fast enough." Ailsa slid a mug of tea onto Kali's desk and perched on the edge. "Here you are, dear. You'll need this."

Kali ran her finger along the list. "So…how do you think I should work it? Brodie's insisting on staying for the next few days, while Callum's still in Intensive Care."

"He's not in Recovery yet?" Ailsa's eyes widened.

"No. He's been in and out of surgery for the past two days." She cleared her throat, trying to keep the emotional fallout at bay. "And this morning Brodie was pretty concerned about his blood pressure. Callum lost a lot of blood before they got him into hospital with the arterial bleed and they were talking about bringing him back into sur—" She choked on the word, unable to continue.

"Hey, now. Our Callum's strong as an ox. If anyone can pull through it's that lad." Ailsa pulled her up and into a warm hug. "Brodie tells me you were an absolute rock. That he couldn't have got through the past couple of days without you."

Kali pulled back, tears streaming down her face. "He said that?"

"'Course he did, love." Ailsa reached across the desk and tugged a tissue out of the ever-present box and handed it to her. "And if I were a betting woman I would guess things are running a bit deeper than that."

Kali felt red blossom on her cheeks.

Ailsa laughed. "I might be well into middle age, darlin', but do you think I haven't seen the sparks between you two?"

"It's not— Well, it's…"

Of all the times to be at a loss for words!

"It is what it is," Ailsa filled in for her. "But you be careful. This is quite a time of turmoil for Brodie, and I love my nephew to bits but I've never known him to be into much of anything for the long-term except for his work."

A fresh wave of tears threatened to spill over onto Kali's cheeks.

"Ach, away." Ailsa pulled her in tight again for a lovely maternal hug. "I'm not saying Brodie will let you down. I'm just saying mind your heart. We've all really taken to you and we'll hate to see you go."

"Brodie's actually asked me to stay on."

"As a partner in the clinic? He'd been talking about it before you came, but I didn't think he meant it." A look of happy disbelief overtook Ailsa's features. "Are you *sure* we're talking about my Brodie? The errant nephew of mine who won't commit to dinner in a couple of hours' time—that Brodie?"

"The very same. But—" Kali quickly covered herself, not wanting to get too excited. "He wasn't specific about the clinic. I presume he just meant until Callum's out of hospital and things are back to normal."

"There's no such thing as 'normal' for Brodie, Callum *or* Dunregan for that matter, love."

Kali's brain was pinging all over the place. And her heart was thudding so loudly she was surprised it wasn't boinging out through her jumper, cartoon-style.

"Are you saying it's best if I leave?"

"Oh, heavens no!" Ailsa looked horrified. "Absolutely not, Kali, love. I'm just an interfering auntie. What happens between you and Brodie is none of my business. You're about the best thing that has happened to him ever since the poor lad's mother died. I'm only saying he's never been settled here. Not in his heart. But these past few weeks I've seen you take to the community here like a duck to water." She sighed. "I suppose I'm saying make sure you know what you want. Brodie and the island don't necessarily come as a package."

Kerthunk.

Could hearts defy the most intricate internal structuring and actually plummet to the pit of your stomach?

That was what it felt like. A best day and a worst day colliding midchest and sinking like a lead weight. Taking all of the air in her chest with it.

Kali looked down at the list of names she'd compiled on her desk, feeling genuine fatigue creeping in and replacing the positive energy that had been keeping her afloat.

Brodie had asked her to stay! Not as his wife or anything, but he'd asked her to *stay*. And here was a list of people all willing to help him as he transitioned from globe-trotter to islander. A *list*! A list in black-and-white of at least two dozen people who'd rung her up this morning, volunteering to take stints of time with Callum so Brodie could get some rest.

She pulled the papers off the desk and forced a bright smile. "I guess we'd better get cracking on putting this rota together before the patients start coming. There's a busy day ahead."

"That there is," Ailsa agreed. She knocked her knuckles against the door frame, as if chiding herself. "Don't let me get you down, Kali. I'm just an overcautious Scot. You might be pleased to hear that Johnny was looking to head over to the mainland soon, to stand in for Brodie so he can come back and get a fresh change of clothes."

Kali's eyes lit up, but she did her best to contain her smile as Ailsa disappeared out into the corridor.

Perhaps Ailsa was right. She wasn't being cautious enough. Wasn't looking after the heart she'd so hoped to set free up here on this beautiful, wild island.

She closed her eyes and there was Brodie, clear as day. All tousled hair and full lips parting in that smile that never failed to send her insides into a shimmy or seven. She guessed it was time to venture into unknown territory yet again, because closing her heart to Brodie... An impossibility.

* * *

"C'mon. Budge over. I need a bit of normal." Brodie pulled a chair up next to Kali's as she looked through the afternoon's patients, wanting to make sure she'd crossed her i's and dotted her t's…or was it the other way round? Brodie must be just as tired as she was. It had taken four days for Callum to get out of ICU. He had been lucky, his doctors had cautioned. *Very* lucky.

She pulled a folder from the top of her ever-growing pile and scanned it.

"All right, then, Doctor. How's about a 'normal' case of toe fungus?" She hung air quotes round the *normal*.

"If it's who I think it is…" Brodie flashed her a quick smile "…it's perfectly normal."

She held up the file so he could see.

"Bingo! Got it in one!" Brodie clapped his hands together happily. "That chap needs to develop a better friendship with his washer-dryer."

"Or just buy some fresh boots and start over?"

They laughed, not unkindly, while Kali made a couple of notes, then moved on to the next patient.

Together they worked through the dozen or so patient files—Brodie offering a bit of insight here, Kali making her usual meticulous notes. The atmosphere between them was perfect. Warm. Companionable. No—even better than that. *Loving.*

She could've sat there all day with him, doing

her best to keep the odd hits of panic at bay. Panic that what she was feeling whenever they were together wasn't real. Panic that she didn't deserve such happiness.

Ailsa's words kept echoing in her head... *Brodie and the island don't necessarily come as a package.*

"When are you going to be done?" Brodie's sotto voce tone sent shivers down her spine as his hands spread out across her back in search of her bra strap. "I want to get you up on the exam table and do some examining of my own."

"Someone's in a good mood." Kali nudged him away with her elbow while she tried to input some information into the computer system.

"Someone's too busy working to indulge me," he teased, tickling her side to no effect.

He sat back in his chair and assessed her.

"Someone else is ignoring very important paperwork." Kali didn't want to be under the microscope right now. Not with the zigzags of emotions she was experiencing.

"Are you putting patient care over your—?" He stopped for a moment, his eyes flicking up to the left in the telltale sign that he was searching for the right thing to say.

"My what?" Kali asked, trying her absolute, very, very best to keep her tone light.

"Boyfriend sounds stupid, doesn't it? And part-

ner always sounds too clinical for me. Too busi-
nessy."

Brodie turned her round in her wheelie chair
and tugged her closer toward him so that he could
lay a deeply satisfying, sexy-as-they-come kiss
on her lips.

Uh-oh! Boy, was she in trouble!

He pulled back and feigned a detached inspection, silently chewing a few words round in his
mouth before sounding them out into her office.

Seafaring Lothario, main squeeze and *plus one*
were rejected outright. "Man-friend?" he tried,
to Kali's resolute horror.

"Or…" He pulled back even farther, eyes
firmly glued on hers. "You don't look entirely
happy, here. Have I jumped the gun?"

"No!" Kali all but shouted, then forced herself to turn her own volume down. "No, I think
it's sweet."

"Sweet?" Brodie recoiled. "I thought you liked
me because I was all silent and broody and mus-
cly. A pensive Viking."

"Oh, definitely!" Kali was giggling now, fears
laid to rest. At least for now. "You're my pensive
Viking."

"You don't have a whole string of us out there,
do you?" Brodie pulled her in again, dropping
kiss after kiss on her lips. "A doctor in every
port?"

"As if."

She returned one of his kisses with the ardor of a Viking mistress whose man had only just returned from months at sea. Shirts became untucked, fingers started exploratory journeys, backs arched, soft moans unfurled out of throats receiving naughty nips and licks as hands squeezed and caressed and—

A knock sounded.

Kali and Brodie hastily tugged everything back into place that should be in place, still giggling when Ailsa opened the door with a wary expression.

"I'm not interrupting anything here, am I?"

"No, Auntie Ailsa. What can we do for you?"

"I've got some patients."

"Already? I thought I had another twenty minutes." Kali's eyes flicked to the clock to double-check.

Ailsa stood back from the door frame and in bounded two very familiar furry beasts, one with a bright pink plaster on her leg.

"Hamish! Dougal!" Kali dropped to her knees, only to be covered in big slobbery kisses.

She'd been visiting the vet's on a daily basis, sending photos to Brodie to show to Callum to prove that Ethel's—now his—beloved dogs were being taken care of.

"Glad to see it's such a happy reunion." Ailsa smiled down at her, before squaring her gaze with Brodie's. "Now, you're sure you're all right to have these two massive bear cubs running round your house until your brother is well enough to look after them?"

"Definitely." Brodie nodded solidly whilst Ailsa's stern expression remained unchanged.

"I know Kali's willing to help, and we can rely on her, but the onus is on *you*, Master McClellan. No swanning off to Africa, or whatever exotic location takes your fancy, with these two relying on you."

Brodie looked down at the two dogs, their big eyes now locked on him. Hopeful. Gleaming. And between them, of course, was Kali. The most beautiful face in the world. Her green eyes were filled with the same glint of hopeful anticipation. One that cemented his decision.

"Yes, Aunt Ailsa." He nodded soberly. "You have my word."

"Well, then…" She gave a brisk *that's done* swipe of her hands. "That's good enough for me. Now, will you be bringing them to Ethel's funeral? I'm fairly certain Callum said she stipulated in her will that they be there."

"That's this Friday, isn't it?" Kali asked, her arms still around her new furry companions.

Ailsa nodded.

"It's a shame it's so soon. Callum would've been the best one to speak."

"Could we get him to do a video link on someone's phone or tablet?" Kali suggested.

"That's a good idea." Brodie nodded as the idea took shape. "Or maybe—as we can't do the pyre until Ethel has been cremated—we could wait until he's back. Even if he's on crutches or in a wheelchair we can wheel him down to the beach before we set the boat alight."

"I'm sorry?" Kali looked like she was choking on the image he'd painted.

"Didn't Callum tell you?"

"The last time I saw him he was so high on painkillers he mostly talked about putting Ethel in a boat and setting it on fire, then shoving it out to sea. I thought he was just away with the faeries."

"Nope. Not in the slightest." Brodie shook his head, and his aunt nodded along with him. It was one of the island traditions he had actually always loved. A traditional Viking funeral. "It won't be completely traditional, because I think Health and Safety have something to do with it. But Ethel requested that her ashes be put out to sea Viking-style. I think she traced her lineage back to the Norse gods, or something mad, and she always was a bit of an old battle-ax…"

An idea shot through him like a jolt of electricity.

"What if I got some of the lads to help me finish my boat and we used that instead of one of those smaller model-types? It would take a couple of weeks, and that would hopefully buy Callum the time to get out of hospital."

"Oh, no—Brodie. Not that one." Ailsa shook her head disapprovingly.

"Why not?" He looked between the two astonished women as if it was perfectly obvious that he should send his handcrafted boat out in a burning pyre of flames.

"Don't worry, ladies. Leave it with me. Ethel will go out in style!"

"Mmm…this is my favorite part of the day." Kali stretched luxuriously, using Brodie as ballast for her small frame as she twisted and wiggled herself from early-morning sleepy to fresh-faced awake.

"And why's that, my sweet little raven-haired minx?" Brodie had a pretty good idea why, but he wanted to hear Kali say it anyhow.

"Calm before the storm."

"Which storm is that? The patients who can't get enough of you? The boatbuilding brigade? The two larger-than-life dogs we've been looking after until my softie of a brother can walk again? Do you want me to keep going?" he asked when she started giggling.

"I don't see them as storms—they're just… life."

"You're *my* calm." Brodie tugged her in so he could give her a smooch on the forehead.

"Hardly!" Kali protested, accepting the kiss anyway, tiptoeing her fingers up along his stomach until they came to rest on his chest. "Does that make you the storm?"

"It's not as if I've brought much tranquility into your life."

They both laughed as Brodie began to tick off the number of things that had happened since his return to Dunregan, and Kali dismissed each of them as insignificant.

"If you'd actually *had* Ebola this would've been a very short-lived romance."

"That's true. And you'd have had to die as well, since we've been snogging ourselves silly."

"How very *Romeo and Juliet* of us!"

"Except my family doesn't hate your family because you keep them all secret and locked up in your little Kali hideaway," Brodie teased.

He felt Kali instantly stiffen beside him. Bull's-eye on the sore subject, and he hadn't even been trying!

He propped himself up on an elbow and drew a finger along her jawline, compelling her to meet his gaze. "Sweetheart…I don't know why you don't talk about your family, but if you ever need to talk about it—about them—we both know you've helped me a lot with mine…"

Kali put on an impish grin—one that didn't

make it all the way to her eyes—gave him a quick peck on the lips and then skittered out from under his arms.

"We've got to get a move on. I want to get the dogs walked before I go to the clinic." She wrapped herself up in his hugely oversized dressing gown, looking like a terrycloth princess in her ceremonial robes. "Today's the big day."

"Ethel's ceremony! And getting Callum back from hospital, of course. Do you think we should make up the downstairs bedroom for him or just let him bed down with the dogs?"

Kali smirked at him and pointed at the linen cupboard down the hallway.

"Well, we'd best crack on, love." He shooed her out of the bedroom. "Hie thee to the shower, lassie. I'll not have you entering the clinic smelling like anything less than a dewy rose."

Brodie fell back into the pile of pillows when he heard the shower go on, glad to have put a smile back on Kali's face. He'd let it slide this time. But now that he realized what an idiot he'd been to turn his back on his family he really hoped she would open up to him about hers. Good or bad, they were worth coming to terms with.

He'd thought he didn't need his family. What had never occurred to him was how much they'd needed *him*. They hadn't been trying to suffocate him. They'd just been trying to love him. And for the first time since his mum had passed he was beginning to believe he was *worthy* of their love.

Just a few days more and he would find out if he was worthy of Kali's.

He rolled over to the far side of the bed and tugged open the drawer of the bedside table, where he'd hidden the tiny green box he'd brought back from the mainland after his last trip to see Callum. He flicked open the box and smiled… one perfect solitaire. All that was left to do now was find the perfect moment.

"Are you sure you're comfortable?" Kali tucked an extra blanket over Callum's knees. Tartan, of course. Over the tartan of his kilt.

"I'm not geriatric. I'm simply…transitioning to bionic. It's a process," Callum grumbled good-na-turedly, swatting her hands away. "If that brother of mine could learn to steer this thing better I might not have shouted so loud when we hit that bump."

"What's that about my driving?"

Brodie sidled up, also kilted-out to the nines, slipping a warming arm across Kali's shoulders. She loved the "everydayness" of the gesture. How protected she felt. Secure.

"Your driving is absolutely wonderful, big brother." Callum grinned.

"That's what I thought you were saying. How's the leg?"

"As I was saying to the beautiful Dr. O'Shea—"

"Hey, watch it," Brodie interrupted, his fingers protectively tucking Kali a bit more possessively under his arm. "I saw her first."

"I know...I know!" Callum held his hands up in the surrender pose. "Seriously, though. Thanks to you two and your stellar calls on my leg, I want you to know I am *feeling* bionic. Even if it will take six months to test run all the new hardware inside it. You'll get front-row seats to the inaugural run, if you can bear looking after me that long."

"Don't worry, Callum. We'll be here to watch you take the first tenuous steps all the way to your first hill run." He gave Kali's arm a little rub. "Won't we, love?"

Kali smiled and nodded, hiding as best she could the hint of anxiety this glimpse into their mutual future had unleashed. She had never planned for the future. Never been able to. The fact that she'd made it through medical school was little short of a miracle.

And her little-girl hopes of falling in love and marrying the man of her dreams one day... Her father had shown her just how much of a nightmare that sort of dream could become.

"Hey, you." Brodie nestled in to give her a peck on the cheek. "Everything all right?"

"Absolutely." She gave him a wide smile. One filled with every ounce of gratitude that she had for having him in her life at all. "I was just thinking—do we have your brother parked in the best place to give his eulogy?"

"Celebratory remembrance, Kali! Ethel would've hated the idea of a eulogy," Callum cut in. "And here was me, worried you'd put me at the end of the dock so Brodie could push me off. What do you think, Kali? You've got to know this wayward beast over the past couple of months… are his intentions honorable?"

Her eyes widened and zipped from Callum's to Brodie's. One set of cornflower-blue eyes was filled with laughter, whilst Brodie's… Was that panic she saw? Whatever it was, it sent her stomach churning.

"Relax, Kali. I'm just messing with you." Callum laughed heartily. "Wow! Take a look at the crowds. I don't think I've ever seen the beach this crowded. Do you think I'll be needing a microphone?"

"Don't worry, little brother. Your dulcet tones are plenty loud enough."

Brodie would've punched his brother's lights out if he hadn't already been laid up in a wheelchair. Trust him to near enough let the cat out of the bag before he'd even had a chance to propose. It wasn't as if Kali had professed her undying love for him or anything. Or said she wanted to stay on Dunregan forever. Something he could picture himself doing. Especially tonight.

He finally saw what his father had wanted him to see. A place where people came together to help. Yes, they knew your secrets, and whether or not your shortbread was better or worse than the woman's next door. But they were a united front in the face of adversity and—in tonight's case—the celebration of a life fully lived. People were absolutely flooding the broad arc of a beach.

Tall torches were secured in the sand every five meters or so, the flames adding a warm glow to the scene. Up above them the stars were out in force, and even though it was freezing cold he felt warmer in his heart than he had in years. Being here with the woman he loved, his brother and his extended family—virtually the entire population of Dunregan—all gathered together to send off Ethel Glenn in about the most dramatic fashion possible. It was heaven-sent.

Kali lit the first candle on Callum's say-so. The atmosphere was hushed, a mix of tears and laughter as everyone remembered Ethel in their own way after Callum gave a simple but loving speech in memory of the woman who had touched each of their lives—if not with her deep understanding of the island, then with her excellent command of shortbread.

Within minutes the sky was filled with scores

of Chinese lanterns. Hamish and Dougal each raised their furry head to the skies and howled their farewells.

"Brodie?" Callum prompted, when a few moments had passed and another collective silence was upon them. "Will you do the honors?"

Brodie stepped forward, his eyes solidly on the boat he had built with the unfettered help of the community. Young and old had gathered to craft her, and for just an instant he felt remorse at the decision to set her alight. But there'd be time to build another one. And he couldn't think of a more appropriate send-off for a woman who had embodied the very essence of the place he was now proud to call home.

"This boat—*The Queen Ethel*—she's a project that's been—" He stopped, feeling the choke of emotion threatening to overwhelm him.

He looked to Kali and gathered the strength he needed from her beautiful green eyes and warm smile.

"This boat was built by many hands. The wood—grown on Dunregan, ordered by my father—has been lovingly crafted—"

"You mean put together with sticky tape?" Johnny shouted from the crowd.

A ripple of laughter lifted the mood, bringing a smile to Brodie's lips.

"Near enough, mate. That and plenty of glue. A thank-you is definitely required for Johnny's long-suffering wife, Helen, for keeping all of us chaps in bridies, scones and raspberry jam for the duration."

He patted his air-inflated stomach, to the delight of the crowd.

"But seriously—and I do mean this from the bottom of what most of you know to be my very wayward heart—this boat would not exist without all of you."

He reached out to Kali and gave her hand a squeeze, buying himself a moment to swallow another surge of emotion.

"We all know I couldn't think of enough reasons to leave this island as a teen—but, having seen the world and come back home…I can assure you all that Ethel exemplified all of the reasons to stay. Will you all charge your glasses, please, as we offer up a toast and a farewell to our dear friend, Ethel Glenn?"

Callum handed Brodie the flaming torch he'd been holding throughout his brother's speech. Brodie raised it aloft as the sound of bagpipes began. Another man untied the boat and with an almighty shove set her out to sea, with the torch Brodie flung in the very center of the craft.

Collectively everyone held their breath as a huge whoosh of flame took hold of the boat and it was transformed into an otherworldly Viking craft.

Huzzahs and shouts of delight filled the air,

and for a few moments Kali stood spellbound by the sight of the boat floating out to sea. By the contrast of the billowing flames reaching up to the heavens and the foamy crash of waves against the hull of the boat.

Out of the corner of her eye she saw motion. An awful lot of motion. Her eyes shifted closer to the shore.

Was that…?

Were those…?

Had they really…?

Her fingers flew to her mouth in disbelief.

Scores of islanders were flinging off their clothes and jumping—some in old-fashioned swimsuits, others completely stark naked—into the sea! Including, she saw with complete amazement as a kilt landed in her arms, Brodie!

Kali laughed and laughed. She'd heard all sorts of people mention the Polar Bear Club, but until this very minute she'd had no idea what they were talking about. With all the white bums bobbing about in the sea, children and adults alike shrieking with delight at the frigid arctic temperatures, the scene had the undeniable feel of a party.

Ethel's boat was quite a distance out now, the fire illuminating the effervescence of the waves with a golden tinge. Completely magical.

Kali could imagine living here until the end of time. Yes, there would always be a hole in her heart where her mother and sister had lived.

Maybe over time she could make it a warmer place. A sacred place where she kept them safe, preserved in a time before she'd known the cruel twists life could sometimes take.

"Here you are, love. Mind giving me a hand?" Ailsa materialized by her side with an enormous bag overflowing with huge fluffy towels.

"Wow! Did a spa go out of business or something? These look amazing!"

"We held a charity do a couple of years back, after folk kept misplacing their towels along the beach. This way the swimmers come out, they towel off, get a warm drink—see the table set up over there by the shore?—and everything goes down to the pub for washing the next day."

"The pub?"

"Aye, they've got one of those big industrial washing machines because of the rooms and the little cabins they let over the summer. That was their donation. Scrubs and suds."

Kali grinned at the wording. If it was possible for her to like Dunregan even more, it was happening.

She stopped for a second, shifting up her chin as if it would help her hear better. Just out of earshot she heard a sharp, frightened call. A woman.

"Jack!" shouted the voice. *"Jaaaack!"*

Kali knew that tone.

Fear.

Complete and utter fear.

CHAPTER TEN

FROM WHERE SHE STOOD, atop the pier, Kali quickly linked the voice with a woman, eyes frantically scanning the sea and the crowded beach, her voice growing more and more strained amidst the loud party atmosphere.

The atmosphere which had just seemed so festive turned abruptly discordant.

The sea water would be warmer than the air—which was just hovering at freezing—but Kali knew cold water like that could kill a child in seconds.

"Ailsa…" She touched her arm and whispered, "Can you go help that woman there? Search along the beach for her child. I'll look in the water."

Ailsa's eyes widened with understanding and she quickly ran down to the beach, pulling people along with her as she went, somehow mysteriously silencing the bagpipes along the way.

Kali forced herself to remain steady, her eyes systematically working along the first few meters of the shoreline.

"Take the dogs." Callum's voice cut through her concentration.

"Sorry?"

"Ethel's dogs," Callum repeated, handing her the leashes. "They're water rescue dogs."

Of course! That would explain why Ethel had been heading to the loch in the dead of winter to "play" with her dogs.

A siren sounded, bringing the whoops and chatter to a complete halt.

Kali's eyes flicked back to Callum.

"That's the lifeboat rescue siren."

"Who's in charge?"

"Johnny. He probably set the siren off. Go." Callum shooed her away. "I know you want to help."

The cove abruptly became a floodlit area, with shocked faces standing out in sharp relief against the night as they regrouped, turning from revelers into a focused search party. Boats appeared, their searchlights fanning this way and that along the broad reaches of the cove.

The beach spanned a good two or three kilometers. What had seemed a cozy and protected arc shifted into a shadowy, borderless expanse.

"Kali?"

She whirled around at the sound of Brodie's voice. A rush of emotion overwhelmed her heartbeat for an instant when he appeared—safe—towel in one hand, dry suits in the other.

"I'm going out in one of the boats." He rapidly scrubbed the sea out of his hair. "Here's a dry suit. I'd like to take one of the dogs out on the boat with me. The suit will be a bit big, but do you mind suiting up and going with Dougal along the shoreline?"

She nodded, slotting all the information into place. "Absolutely."

Seconds morphed into minutes.

The calling of the little boy's name—Jack was a mischievous four-year-old who'd slipped the protective grip of his mother's hand—rang out again and again.

Kali was hyperaware of how precious each passing moment was. If Jack had run into the water hypothermia was a threat. Children had a higher ratio of surface area to mass than adults, causing them to cool much faster. But there was a plus side. Cold water would instantly force his body to conserve oxygen—it would slow down the heart instead of stopping it and would immediately shift blood to vital parts of the body. The brain. The heart. Particularly in children.

Kali felt a surge of energy charge her as the community turned from being mourners to a mobilized search and rescue team.

"Here. Let me make sure you've got these sealed up properly."

Brodie shifted and tugged the bright orange neoprene suit she'd pulled on, sealing her into a cocoon of body heat. Something that poor little child, if he were in the sea, wouldn't have.

Brodie locked his bright eyes to hers. "Jack's wearing a sky blue puffer jacket. He has hair the color of your suit—all right?" He dropped a distracted kiss on her forehead. "See you soon. Be safe."

"You, too," she whispered to his retreating figure, extra glad for the company of the warm shaggy dog beside her.

"Right, Dougal." She gave his head a good rub. "Let's go to work."

Kali saw him at a distance, and Dougal made the same link a lightning-fast second later. She blew on her whistle as hard as she could and ran so fast her lungs burned with the exertion.

Jack was farther down the beach than she would've believed possible. Whether he'd been caught in a crosscurrent or had wandered off and then been sucked under by a wave they'd probably never know. All that mattered now was getting the tiny figure out of the water.

Dougal reached Jack, instantly grabbing a hold of the hood of his coat. Kali swam as hard as she could. The tide was stronger than she'd anticipated, but she got there. Her toes were unable to touch the sea floor. Jack's pallor was a deathly blue white. It was impossible to check his pulse, but she knew he was hovering somewhere between life and death.

She took the life ring attached to Dougal's

safety line and got it round Jack as best she could, ensuring his head was above water, blowing her whistle again and again in between choking on mouthfuls of briny seawater.

Just when her toes had managed to gain purchase on the sea floor she saw Brodie arriving, poised at the helm of a speedboat, its searchlight all but blinding her. With a Herculean effort, and a well-placed nose-nudge from Dougal, she managed to hoist the little boy out of the water and into Brodie's waiting arms.

Someone else's arms reached out to pull her in. She waved off the offer, needing to slosh through the water back to the shore. Just a few minutes alone, to walk off the shakes of adrenaline now shuddering through her.

The speedboat whizzed off to the pier, where a team of people were already on standby to receive the tiny patient.

Something in her gut told her the boy would live.

Something in her heart clicked into a place she'd long dreamed of.

She knew where she belonged.

She was irrevocably part of the island now. Sea, sand, sky—the entire package felt imbedded in her in a way she'd never believed possible. And she would do everything in her power to hold it tight.

* * *

Brodie checked the boy's pulse again, shaking his head when he felt nothing. "Can someone grab the pelican cases from my four-by-four?" he shouted, to no one in particular.

They appeared by his side moments later, along with a huge pile of dry towels, blankets and clothing. He could see feet jostling and hear the murmur of the crowd shifting and changing, but his focus remained steadfastly on his hands, clasped together, delivering the steady cadence of compressions required to bring Jack's heart back to life.

"The air ambulance is going to be at least an hour. They're just finishing another call. What do you need me to do?"

Kali dropped to her knees on the other side of Jack, the AED in her hands.

"He's not responding. Severe hypothermia. Body temperature twelve degrees below normal." He kept his voice low. The anxious keening of the boy's mother still came in waves of sound above them.

"Twenty-five Celsius? You've got a thermometer that registers temperatures that low?"

Brodie nodded. "Have to up here. Unfortunately this sort of thing isn't unusual."

It was how his mother had died. He more than most knew the importance of warming this child in the safest way possible.

"We need to get some fluids inside him. I don't want to use the defibrillator until we're inside."

"If the ambulance is going to be a while, should we get him to the clinic?"

"Yes, but he's going to need constant CPR." Brodie was panting. He'd already been administering CPR for over ten minutes, and the intensity of his focus was beginning to take a toll. "Can you help me intubate?"

"Absolutely—then let's get him on the biggest backboard we have and I'll ride it."

"I've got a surfboard right here," someone called.

"Great." Brodie nodded. "Get the board." His eyes flicked up to meet Kali's. The steady green gaze assured him that they had this—as a team.

Swiftly, efficiently, they intubated Jack and then transferred him to the board. Kali straddled the small body and took over CPR while Jack compressed the airbag providing oxygen to the little boy's lungs.

"Steady, lads," Brodie cautioned as six men lifted the board on his count. "Precious cargo."

His eyes were on Kali, whose expression was one of utter focus on the child. She was in a class of her own. He would count himself lucky to have had her in his life at all, let alone for the rest of his life. He made a silent promise to propose sooner than later.

"Fluids?" Kali threw him a questioning look.

"Nothing warm enough to put into a drip. Everything will have gone cold in the car."

"Warmer than his body?"

He nodded. It was a good point. They'd have to warm him gradually. Anything else would be too much of a shock to the small body that had already been traumatized.

"All right, lads? Slide them in as steady as you can."

The trip to the clinic passed in a blur of CPR, pulse checks, IV insertion, airway checks and temperature monitoring.

"It's not looking good, is it?" Jack's mother asked tearfully. She was leaning over the seat into the back of the car, where Kali was still carrying out CPR.

"I read about a case of a two-year-old…" Kali huffed between compressions. "Fell into an icy river—must've been in it for half an hour at least. They performed CPR for over an hour and a half. Between that, fluids and other warming methods they got him back."

"But was he all right? You know…" Jack's mother asked, not wanting to put words to everyone's concern. Irreparable brain damage.

Kali nodded. She thought so, but wasn't 100 percent. She wanted to offer hope, but knew there was a degree of caution required in all hypotheticals.

"We're here," Brodie said unnecessarily as the vehicle slowed to a careful halt.

He'd thrown the keys to one of the lads. CPR was tiring. If Kali needed to be relieved he wanted to be by her side to help.

"Kali, if you grab the IV bag I'll take over."

Again, the concentrated blur of saving someone's life had shifted everything else out of his consciousness. If they could just get…

"We've got a pulse!" Kali finally said, a few minutes after having hooked Jack up to the monitoring system. "It's weak, but we've got one."

A collective sigh of relief released the taut tension in the exam room, where Jack's family had anxiously been looking on.

"Will you be needing the ventilator?" Ailsa appeared in the doorway.

"Thanks, Ailsa. Yes. It'll make it easier for the little guy to breathe, and maybe we can get some aerosol medication in him."

Brodie curled his fingers into a loose fist and gave Jack a quick sternal rub. He felt a twitch of a response. Heard a cough, then a gag.

"Quick! Let's get him in the recovery position."

He and Kali quickly shifted Jack onto his side, a stream of seawater gushing out of the little boy's mouth as they did so, and a wail of relief from his mother filled the room.

They'd done it. They'd brought him back to life.

Kali gave Brodie a happy nod, her lips shifting in and out of her mouth as she tried to keep the emotion at bay. He felt it, too. Deep in his heart. All he wanted to do was pull Kali into his arms, but they weren't out of the woods yet.

"Right, guys. We're still fighting the hypothermia. Anyone have word on that air ambulance?"

Kali gave him a soft smile as a new flurry of activity began to whirl around them. They would do this. Together.

"Look who's on the front page!" Brodie flourished the *Dunregan Chronicle* in front of Kali.

She felt the blood drain from her face in an instant. She could hear Brodie happily chattering away, but his voice was only coming to her in the odd hit of vowels and consonants she couldn't put together. She blinked hard, forcing herself to concentrate on what he was saying.

"Craig thinks it's so good the nationals might pick it up. It's already all over the internet—so some of the international papers might run it."

Her breath came out in short, sharp huffs.

"What's wrong?" Brodie sat down beside her, laying the paper down on the round table in front of her. "I think it's an amazing shot. You should be proud."

"I am—it's not that—I just…"

She stared at the photograph in disbelief. A picture of the moment she and Dougal had hoisted the near-lifeless body of little Jack into the lifeboat was printed in full color—her face was utterly unmistakable. She was struck by the confidence, the passion she saw in herself. The complete antithesis of the fear she felt welling within her now.

"Hey, babe." Brodie slid a hand across her back in a slow circular motion. "What's wrong with being the heroine of Dunregan for a day? It's well deserved."

"Everything!" The word came out as a wail as years of fear came to the fore. Hot tears poured down her cheeks, and the back and forth *no, no, no* shaking of her head flicked them onto the paper, instantly blurring the ink.

"Kali, you're scaring me. What's going on?"

She turned to him, knowing that this might be one of the last moments when Brodie's belief in her was absolute. The moment she'd been dreading had finally arrived. The moment when she had to explain to Brodie that the Kali he knew... was a fiction.

"Come here."

He held open his arms but she couldn't move. The weight in her heart was rendering her motionless except for her head, which persisted with its shaking. *No, no, no.*

"Right." Brodie pushed back from the table and headed toward the kitchen counter. "I'm making you a fresh cup of tea—and then, Kali O'Shea,

you are going to tell me exactly what has got
you so—"

"I'm not Kali O'Shea."

The words were blurted out before she could
stop them and they seemed to assault Brodie
physically. His blue eyes clouded, steady blinks
shuttering them from her view every few seconds, and his body became absolutely rooted to
the spot.

"Who are you, then?"

Ice water ran through her veins. All she could
hear in Brodie's voice was the betrayal he had to
be feeling. She pressed her fingers together to
stop their shaking and forced herself to tell him
the story.

"My birth name is Aisha Kalita."

Brodie folded his arms across his chest, as if
protecting himself from what she was about to
say. She didn't blame him. This was a blindsider.
A trust breaker. So it was now or never if she was
going to win his trust again.

"My father is originally from India. He is…
very *traditional*…"

In a monotone, Kali heard herself telling Brodie about her naively happy childhood, the support her parents had given her in her quest to
become a doctor.

"So what happened?"

"He arranged a marriage for me. My father."

"What?" Brodie all but shouted the word.

The dogs came scrambling in from the lounge, where they had been lolling in the morning sun, big furry heads shifting from Brodie to Kali, waiting to see who needed them most.

Kali sat rigidly as Brodie digested the news, her hand distractedly giving each of the dog's heads a rub.

"Sorry, Kali. Please. Go on."

The clinical tone of his voice sent another chill of fear through her. She swallowed and forced herself to tell the story that had been told out loud only once, five years earlier at the Forced Marriage Protection Unit.

"My father had been planning it for months, but none of us knew about it. Not my mother or sister—"

"You have a sister?"

She shook her head yes, and continued. If she didn't get it all out now…

"It was someone from my father's hometown. A man highly esteemed for his business acumen—but not for his morals. My father organized for me to marry this man and secured a visa for him in England."

She choked back a sob.

Brodie came toward her, stopping himself halfway, as if undecided about whether or not to comfort her. Her heart physically hurt. For him, for herself, for the lies she'd been forced to tell and for the life she'd thought she could have.

She put up a hand. "Please. Let me finish."

He pulled out a chair on the opposite side of the table and nodded for her to continue. It was impossible to tell what was happening behind those pure blue eyes of his. She prayed to everything she could think of that he would be empathic. Compassionate. Forgiving.

"I was completely clueless. My father brought him over to dinner one day and then later made my sister and mother leave the room with him so that it was just the two of us. He wasted no time in telling me how the marriage would work. Who would be in charge. That I would have to shelve my medical degree and do something more… something that would give me more time to look after him. When I protested and said I would only go ahead with the marriage if I were able to complete my medical studies he—"

A ragged sob escaped her very core.

"He hit me. The rest of it happened horribly fast. My father was in the room in an instant, apologizing—can you believe it?—*apologizing* to this man for my behavior. When he left I begged my father to be released from the union. He said the only way I could escape the marriage—humiliating him as I had—was death."

Brodie's hand shot across the table. He needed to touch her. Comfort her. Aisha… Kali—whatever her name was—she was the same woman she'd been ten minutes ago. If there was any way he could have taken back his initial reaction he would have.

Kali slid her own hand across the table, then retracted it.

"What happened next?" Part of him didn't want to know, but it was imperative he heard the full story.

"In the middle of the night my mother came to me with a small amount of money and an address for a distant relative in Ireland. She said I should seek her out if I absolutely must—but if it were possible to just go. Never speak of them or think of them again."

In a rush she blurted out the rest. The tremors of fear juddering through her body as she'd stuffed a handful of clothes into a small backpack. The fearful silence in the house as they'd tiptoed to the back door, terrified of waking her father. The tears she'd been unable to shed as she'd hugged her sister and mother goodbye that one last time.

"And then I just began to run."

Brodie itched to hold her. Ease away the pain. But she had to finish. He could see the determination in her eyes.

"I stayed at a cheap hostel the first night. And then—because I didn't want anyone to know where I was, especially if my father was going to go on the hunt for me—I spent my days in

London's biggest hospitals. Just reminding myself why I had chosen to become a doctor. I spent my nights in the waiting room of an ER until a nurse finally figured out something was wrong and helped me contact the Forced Marriage Protection Unit. They helped me with a new identity. But with the invention of Kali O'Shea I had to let my mother and sister go."

Brodie felt his throat go dry, his body physically aching for her. He'd left his family of his own accord. A selfish decision by a teenager blinded with grief and anger after a tragic accident. But Kali...? She'd been betrayed by her own father and forced to live apart from the people who could have comforted her most.

"And you've never been back?"

"Never." Her eyes were wide with disbelief, though she was the one who'd lived with the pain, the reality of a life lived in fear. "I moved to Dublin so I could feel close to my mother's relatives. It was a weak link—but it helped, believe it or not."

"That's why you picked the name O'Shea?"

"No." Kali finally looked across at him, her beautiful green eyes shining with vitality. "It was the name of the nurse who helped me that night. Helped me to find the FMPU and make a fresh start. Become who I'd always thought I could be."

She was so much braver than he had ever imagined. Stronger.

Brodie couldn't restrain himself anymore. He

was pulling her into his arms before he could stop himself, running his fingers through her hair, holding her tight to his chest so she could weep long pent-up tears of grief, fear and loss.

"My beautiful, brave Kali...Aisha," he corrected, then laughed awkwardly. "What do you want me to call you?"

"Kali," she answered without hesitation. "It's the name I chose because I thought it would give me strength. And it has. And," she added, looking at him as if she hardly believed he was still there, "I *have* become who I thought I could be. Thanks to you, to Ailsa—everyone here on Dunregan."

"But mostly me, right?" he teased gently.

"Mostly you." Her fingers pressed into his.

"You've never looked for them? Your family?" Brodie asked, leading her out to the sofa in the lounge, where they nestled into a big pile of humans, dogs and cushions.

"I was far too frightened the first couple of years. There were enough scary stories of retribution killings to keep me as far away from my father as I could. Though I worry about my mum and sister. Every day I worry that my father turned his anger on them."

She shook her head, suddenly looking overwhelmed with exhaustion.

"Are you—are you okay with this? With me?"

"Are you kidding?" Brodie shook his head in

disbelief. "Obviously it's all a bit of a shock, but I love you, Kali. I don't think having a different name changes who you are and what you mean to me."

Kali blinked, her teeth biting endearingly into her lower lip as she did so. "You *love* me?"

"Of course I do. What did you think? I go parading around Dunregan with every beautiful woman who shows up here?"

"I—uh—"

"Don't answer that." Brodie laughed, scooching along the sofa so he could hold her in his arms. "I love you, Kali O'Shea, and I will do everything in my power to ensure you're never put in harm's way. You have my word."

He dropped a kiss onto the top of her head, enjoying the weight of her body as she slowly let herself relax into his embrace.

They were words he'd never said to a woman before.

I love you.

And they were words he meant from the bottom of his heart. The only thing left to do was rustle up the most romantic setting he could and propose.

"Kali?"

It was Brodie, gently knocking on the door to her office.

"You left your mobile in the staff room and it

rang. I hope you don't mind, but I answered it for you."

"Who is it?"

A jag of fear ran through her. It had been twenty-four hours since the photo had gone public and she'd heard nothing so far.

"Is it a man or a woman?" she whispered, more to herself than Brodie. She would never forget the malice in her father's voice. Not as long as she lived.

"A woman," Brodie said with a smile, his blond hair shining in the late-morning sun coming through the back door. "I think you'll want to take it. It's a Mrs. Kalita."

Tears leaped to her eyes as one set of fingers popped to her lips and the other to her chest, as if trying to hold her heart inside.

Her entire body shook with anticipation as she reached forward to accept the phone from Brodie. She had to hold it with both her hands as she took it from him, the tremor in her fingers was so strong.

Over five years. It had been over five painfully long years.

Brodie took a step back, dismay furrowing his brow. He mouthed a question. *Want me to stay?*

She shook her head, no, then quickly changed it to yes. Brodie was part of her life now. No more secrets.

She took a big breath and lifted her fingers off

the phone's mouthpiece. "Hello?" Her voice was barely audible.

"Aisha?" The familiar name came down the line, the voice causing her tears to spill over. "Aisha, is this connection all right? Can you hear me?"

Kali nodded silently, only just remembering to speak the word she hadn't allowed herself to say out loud for over half a decade…

"Mummy-ji?"

CHAPTER ELEVEN

KALI SET DOWN the phone in disbelief.

She was free!

She felt herself go into autopilot—stepping away from her desk, only just remembering to give Brodie's hand a little squeeze, blindly taking the handful of steps to the small kitchen, filling the kettle, listening to it come to a boil as she had on her very first day here.

She watched, almost as if she were someone else, as her hands reached for mugs, opened the tea canister, fingers deftly, knowingly, going about making cups of tea for everyone. An extra splash of milk for Ailsa, a sugar-even-though-she-knew-she-shouldn't for Caitlyn, strong builder's tea for herself and, of course, leaving the tea bag in the longest for Brodie, and adding just a few drops of milk…one…two…three…four.

Four weeks.

Four weeks of living on the sanctuary of Dunregan. Embracing the life here every bit as much as it had embraced her. And now she could just… go…?

"Hey, you."

Brodie slipped into the tearoom behind her. Kali felt the warmth of his hands shifting along her hips and lacing loosely around her waist. The inevitable tremor of desire skittered down her spine as he nestled into the crook of her neck to give her a smattering of soft kisses along her neck.

She murmured instinctively, tipped her head toward his, loving his scent, his touch, the fact that she knew how to make his tea and which side of the bed he slept on—and the instant she turned around to clink mugs with him felt a cascade of tears begin to pour down her face.

"Oh, hey, now…" Brodie's face was wreathed in concern. "What did she say?"

He took Kali's mug of tea and set it on the counter.

"It's my parents…my family," she choked out as the wash of tears grew thicker.

"So that was her?" His voice tightened, concern woven through each word. "Your mother?"

She managed a nod.

"And…?" He tugged a hand through his hair, losing his knit cap in the process, his eyes completely locked on her. "Kali, are they—have they been hurt in any way?"

She shook her head, no, and forced herself to calm down. Happiness came in so many forms, and the flood of tears streaming freely down her cheeks were tears of pure joy.

At last.

"They're safe." She hiccuped and laughed. "Sorry, it's just…"

"Pretty overwhelming?" Brodie finished for her.

She nodded, and blew out a slow breath before beginning to explain what she'd just learned from her mother. "They're living in Ireland, near the village where her relatives are. My sister's great. She's—" Her eyes filled with tears again. "She's training to be a doctor."

"Like her big sister?" Brodie clapped his hands together.

"Yup." She felt a burst of pride taking shape in her heart, then a shot of sorrow. "My dad…" She shook her head at the enormity of putting all of these sentences together. "My dad…he—he is divorced from my mum and lives in India now. He's become a *monk*."

Her eyes widened in wonder.

"He spent one year solid looking for me, and my mother said the rage and anger all but killed him. He returned home one night and nearly hit my sister when she stood up to him—told him to leave me be. It was then that he broke down, told my mother he just couldn't live with the shame of how he'd behaved. So…now he's a monk in a religious sanctuary somewhere in India."

"So…" Brodie began tentatively. "It's all good?"

"I've just been so scared they wouldn't have

been able to get on with their lives, you know? I so wanted to write to them, tell them to please carry on with everything as if I was still with them, because they were with *me*." She clasped her hands to her heart. "Every step of the way I brought them with me."

"Of course you did." Brodie laid a hand atop of hers, as if to cement what she'd said.

Brodie rubbed his hands along her arms and pulled her in for a hug—but not before she saw a hit of anxiety flash across his face.

She pressed her fingertips into his back, loving the strength of feeling and connection passing between them. Of all the people in the world she could share her news with—the most joyous news she could ever imagine—this was the one she wanted. The man she could imagine a future with.

She felt his chin shift along the top of her head, his hand brushing her hair back from her tearstained face, his fingertips tracing along her jawline before tugging her back into his chest for a tight, long-held embrace. She stood, so grateful just to breathe and listen as their hearts began to beat in synchronicity.

As their breathing shifted and changed, each of them taking on the enormity of the news, she sensed a shift in Brodie's mood. He was happy for her—she didn't doubt that. But there was… She tipped her head up to take a look at his face.

There was anxiety creasing his forehead, shifting the crinkles alongside his eyes into winces of doubt and worry.

"So." Brodie abruptly pulled back from their embrace and put on a bright smile. "I guess this means you'll be leaving us."

"Well, I—" Kali scraped her nails along her scalp, as if it would help clear the jumble of thoughts. "I have to go to them."

"Of course." Brodie nodded as if he were agreeing with a patient about a need to get a second opinion on an unusual condition. "You must."

The coolness in his voice physically chilled her. She knew him well enough to know this was Brodie in protection mode, and as much as it pained her she understood completely. If she had been in his shoes she would have done the same.

"Brodie?" Callum flicked off the television. "Stop pacing, would you? She'll be back."

"It's been over a week now."

"You've texted. And called."

"I know. But everything's going great for her! She's having the time of her life."

"Aren't you happy for her?"

"Of course I am!" Brodie shouted, then checked himself. "Of course I am. It's just…"

What if I never see her again?

"I don't think Kali is the type to just leave a

man hanging," Callum replied calmly, and his voice was an echo of their father's.

Since when had his kid brother become the mature one?

Brodie wheeled around. "What makes *you* so sure?"

Callum's lips twitched as he unsuccessfully held back a snigger.

"Oh, go ahead. Get a good laugh in, why don't you? Enjoy it while you can because—because..." He threw up his hands.

Helpless. He felt absolutely and utterly helpless. Maybe he should go chop wood or something. If he knew where the ax was that was exactly what he would do.

"Brodie..." Callum looked his brother straight in the eye. "You may be many things—but the last thing you are is someone who gives up."

Brodie harrumphed.

Callum laughed openly this time, giving his brother a playful jab with one of his crutches.

"Why don't you go down to the docks?"

"What on earth for?"

"There's a boat coming in." Callum checked his watch. "I have something on there I need you to get."

"So I'm your slave boy now?"

"Hardly!" Callum laughed again. "But I think you'll like this delivery." He aimed the remote at the television, feigning a renewed interest in the show neither of them had been watching. "It'll make you a lot easier to be around, that's for sure."

"What is it? Earplugs so you don't have to listen to me wallowing anymore?"

Callum pushed his lower lip out and jigged his chin back and forth. "Something along those lines. Go." He pointed toward the door. "And take the dogs while you're at it."

"What is it, Dougal?"

Brodie could barely keep a hold of the huge dog's leash as passenger after passenger walked off the boat. Deliveries always came last.

Dougal jumped up with a joyful woof and broke free of Brodie's hold. Hamish dragged Brodie along with him, across the gangplank and onto the boat, where they near enough clobbered someone to the ground. Wagging tails, whines of pleasure—this was no stranger.

"Dogs! What are you—?" Brodie shook his head in disbelief when he caught a glimpse of green eyes amidst the furry bodies. "Kali?"

Flat out on the ferry deck, being covered in dog licks, was Kali, her face wreathed in smiles. Brodie elbowed past the dogs and helped to pull her up, pulling her tightly into his arms.

"What are you doing here?"

She pulled back from the embrace and smiled shyly up at him. "I thought I would come home..."

"Are you asking or telling?" Brodie wasn't going to take any chances here.

"A bit of both, I guess." Kali wove her fingers through his and scooped up one of the dog's leashes, handing him the other. "Fancy a walk on the beach?"

A few minutes later Brodie, Kali and the dogs piled out of the four-by-four onto the beach. The ride had been largely silent. Just two people grinning at each other as if it were Christmas morning. From the deep hits of magnetic connection each of his smiles brought, Kali knew she'd made the right decision.

"So...seeing your family again..." Brodie began tentatively, unlooping the dogs' leashes from around their necks, watching them race out to the shoreline for a swim.

"It was amazing," Kali answered honestly. "My sister is incredible and my mother—strongest woman I know."

A rush of tears filled her eyes. It *had* been amazing. To be with her family. To find the inner peace she'd long sought.

"And how was it to be back in Ireland?"

It was impossible not to hear the worry in Brodie's voice. Worry she never wanted him to feel again. "It was great, because my family is there, but home..." Her lips parted into a broad, hopeful smile. "*This* is home." She scanned the beach, then laid a hand on Brodie's chest. "*You* are home."

She felt the whoosh of release from Brodie's chest.

"I'm pretty happy to hear that."

"Just 'pretty happy'?" She grinned up at him.

"Relieved—over the moon—ecstatic." He threw a few more words out into the ether for added measure until they were both laughing.

He cupped her face in his hands, tilting it up to his for a long-awaited kiss. *Passionate* didn't even begin to cover it. As their lips touched, sparks of desire burst throughout Kali's body. Her arms smoothed along his chest, up and around his neck, and her feet arched up onto tiptoe. She could feel Brodie's arms tighten around her waist, pulling her in close to him, close enough for her to feel his heart racing as fast as her own.

Minutes, hours could have passed for all she was aware. Nothing mattered—nothing existed outside of Brodie.

"I love you, Brodie McClellan." Her lips shifted and whispered across his as she spoke.

"I love you, too, my little one."

He loosened his hold on her, then held her out at arm's length, a serious expression taking over the wash of desire they had both succumbed to.